Supersonic and June

GW00801698

Kevin Lavin was born in Mayo and grew up on a farm near Claremorris. He has worked as an actor, director and writer in Sligo, Galway and Dublin. He has written several plays for children, many of them versions of well-known fairy tales, which have been performed in schools and theatres all over Ireland. He lives in Dublin and works in video production.

Supersonic and June

Kevin Lavin

Illustrated by Áine Duggan

WOLFHOUND PRESS

First published in 1999 by
Wolfhound Press Ltd
68 Mountjoy Square
Dublin 1, Ireland
Tel: (353-1) 874 0354
Fax: (353-1) 872 0207

© 1999 Kevin Lavin

All rights reserved. No part of this book may be reproduced or utilised in any form or by any means digital, electronic or mechanical including photography, filming, video recording, photocopying, or by any information storage and retrieval system or shall not, by way of trade or otherwise, be lent, resold or otherwise circulated in any form of binding or cover other than that in which it is published without prior permission in writing from the publisher.

This book is fiction. All characters, incidents and names have no connection with any persons living or dead. Any apparent resemblance is purely coincidental.

The Arts Council
An Chomhairle Ealaíon
Wolfhound Press receives financial assistance from The Arts Council/An Chomhairle Ealaíon, Dublin, Ireland.

British Library Cataloguing in Publication Data
A catalogue record for this book is available from the British Library.

ISBN 0-86327-718-7

10 9 8 7 6 5 4 3 2 1

Cover illustration: Áine Duggan
Cover design: Slick Fish Design, Dublin
Typesetting: Wolfhound Press
Printed and bound by The Guernsey Press Co., Guernsey, Channel Islands

In memory of Liam Rigney
who took me to see peregrine falcons

Contents

1	The Talisman	9
2	Turkey, Parrot, Pigeon	16
3	Supersonic's Training	26
4	Racing North	37
5	The Dance	48
6	Picnic by the Sea	54
7	The Race of No Return	58
8	The Monster of the Cave	66
9	Follow the Tracks	73
10	Home for a While	79
11	Guardian of the Eyrie	87
12	Nodser	92
13	A Small Space	98
14	Moonflight	102
15	Shahin	116
16	A Brave Deed	130
17	Down by the Docks	141
18	Dance of Love	155

The Talisman

~

When June Corcoran went to see the Indian fortune-teller in the little shopping arcade, she found his premises empty and the arcade deserted. It had once been a warren of second-hand-clothes shops and handmade-jewellery stalls. There was a sign on the glass door of what had been a coffee shop. Sniffily, it reported that:

This arcade is in its present condition
due to the policies pursued by the owners,
Jones, Fox and Co. of ....

— and it gave the address, in case anyone wanted to take the matter up with them.

The arcade was in an archway linking a very busy pedestrian street with a not-so-busy one. June was the only person there. Feeling like she was exploring the ruins of a lost civilisation on whose planet her spacecraft had crash-landed, she approached the fortune-teller's premises. She was able to see past the sign on the window and through the glass door. Today there was no smell of burning incense hanging like a fog outside. And inside there was no red-satin-draped table where Shahin the fortune-teller put his statue of a bird of prey — the statue that all the trouble had been about, last time.

Shahin called the fist-sized statue his talisman. He had told June proudly, the first time she had visited him, that it was a sapphire — a glittering blue gemstone, especially valuable when it was so large.

Whenever June came across a word she didn't understand, she looked it up in her dictionary. Under 'talisman', she found 'object supposed to have magic powers'.

Shahin's method of fortune-telling was to take a Polaroid photograph of each visitor. He would place this flat on the table and hold the talisman over it. Light from the photograph, reflected in the sparkling talisman, enabled him to tell the person's fortune. 'Your fortune is in the bird. Do you see it? Do you see it?' he would ask excitedly.

June never could. She would see shapes that flickered and flew like blue candlelight, but she had to rely on the fortune-teller to make sense of them.

Today all she saw was a brown cardboard box in the middle of the floor. The room's silence and emptiness was almost as mysterious as what had been there in Shahin's time. On the glass door was a sign which said:

Shahin — Dream-Interpreter & Fortune-Teller
Closed due to Unforeseen Circumstances

And it gave an address where he could be contacted. It was miles away. Disappointed, June turned and walked back to the busy shopping street.

June was interested in the future, and she often

imagined what life would be like in a hundred years' time. Sometimes she made up stories about journeys to unexplored worlds in the depths of the starry night sky, which she loved to watch when there was nothing on TV. But today something much closer to home was bothering her, and she had wanted to talk to Shahin about it.

It was a sunny Saturday morning in late March. June had some time to wander around the city centre before getting the bus to Ratheane, where she lived. She also had an extra five pounds in her pocket. She wondered why Shahin charged less for under-16s. You'd think it would be more, because usually they had more future to tell than older people did.

June would be twelve in June. She had been born in June, so her parents had called her June. She had questioned them about this: couldn't they have shown a little more imagination? Her father told her she was lucky they hadn't called her Friday Night.

The second time June had visited Shahin, he had told her of the goddess in ancient Rome who had given her name to the month of June. Ever since, June had been proud of her name.

People were very bright and cheerful this morning, because of the sunshine and the sparkling feeling of spring being near. Most had left their coats at home and were wearing colourful dresses or jackets, jeans and T-shirts. It was easier to see people's faces and shapes than when they were bundled up in winter. Walking down the street was more interesting.

June saw a girl of her own age coming out of a sports shop. The girl had high cheekbones, full lips and dazzling Queen-of-Sheba eyes. Her hair was shoulder-length, black, and had the kind of straightness that only the most expensive stylist can give you, if you don't have it naturally.

June made a mental note: 'People don't earn their faces.' She would write it in her diary when she got home.

It wasn't really a diary — more a notebook where June recorded her thoughts. For instance, yesterday she had had an argument with her friend Jennifer Adams about fortune-telling. Jennifer, who lived next door, thought fortune-telling was nonsense — and dangerous too! June had pointed out that both of them had been to see Shahin six weeks earlier. Jennifer had said that that was why she thought it was nonsense — look at what had happened! (Jennifer had tried to steal the talisman and Shahin had been angry. Very angry.) So, last night, June had written in her notebook, 'You can disagree with people and still be friends.'

This evening it would be, 'People don't earn their faces.' Because June knew the girl with the interesting face. She was Sian Whelan, who lived at the end of June's road, and she was not interesting. People thought she was, because she looked it; but just let them try talking to her about anything other than her Saturday-afternoon drives to the countryside with her mum and dad, and see how they got on. Sian's looks were an accident of nature and very unfair.

June didn't look interesting at all, but she really was. That was even more unfair. For a second she thought she might write, 'People who don't look interesting are,' but then she remembered her brother Gerry. He didn't look interesting — but he wasn't, either. He was probably the most interesting person in the world if all you wanted to talk about was pigeon-racing and motor-bikes; but if you wanted to talk about, say, the sky at night or the advantages of socks made from natural rather than synthetic fibres, then you had a problem. He could play the guitar; but he wouldn't talk about it. Actually, now that June thought about him, Gerry was probably more interesting than a lot of people.

She went into the sports shop. She had avoided Sian Whelan by looking the other way when Sian came out of the shop with her mum. (Sian would never go into the city centre on her own on a Saturday morning.) Sian had been carrying a bulging carrier bag. No doubt June would be told all about the shopping trip at school, but she really didn't feel like poking her head into the bag just then — as Sian and Mrs Whelan would insist she did. Sian's mum was always buying her new rollerblades and designer runners and T-shirts and whatever else Sian took a fancy to.

Mrs Whelan worked in an insurance office. So did Mr Whelan. Sian was forever going on about how her mum and dad had met in the office and fallen in love. Mrs Whelan still couldn't come back from lunch without finding a Kinder Bueno or a Ferrero Rocher from Mr Whelan by her computer. 'And she has the figure to prove it,' June always thought when Sian told her about this.

Security guards up and down the street were muttering into crackling walkie-talkies, and June imagined what they were saying.

'Black-haired girl just gone in, Johnno. Over.'

'Red denim jacket? Chirpy young one? Probably gets freckles in summer? Spotted her, Anto. Over.'

Every time June went into a large shop, she imagined security guards watching her. That woman in the corner, trying on a baseball cap and casually glancing June's way — was she a plain-clothes store detective? June felt like buying something, just to show she wasn't a thief, but there was nothing in the shop to be had for five pounds — not even a baseball cap. Probably this was why most people bought things here. This was why Sian Whelan and her mum had spent maybe three hundred pounds, the silly .... But no — no one would ever think Sian Whelan was a thief. She looked too interesting. Too cool. Too rich. She already had everything you could ever want!

Whenever June was surrounded by an Aladdin's treasure of gleaming rollerblades and space-age runners, a little voice saying 'I want I want I want' switched on in her head. So her thoughts were going like this: *If I had some of those* (I want) *cool runners and* (I want) *rollerblades, I'd look cool* (I want) *too. Then* (I want) *everyone would be just as fascinated by me* (I want) *as they are by Sian Whelan. Even more so, 'cause I know there's more to being interesting, once you've got over the problem of how you look. Like how you speak. Not your accent — that just depends on where you come from — but being able to speak clearly and confidently, and sounding as if you know what you're talking about. I can do that. That purple jacket on the rail!* (I want I want I want ....)

Suddenly it struck June that looking cool and interesting was not an accident of nature. It had to do with having lots of money and wearing the right clothes. You weren't stuck with how you looked.

Figuring things out always made June feel very pleased with herself, and she decided to have some fun. She started to act deliberately suspicious. Glancing over her shoulder, she slipped a designer T-shirt from its hanger and hung around the door as if she was waiting for a chance to run for it. When an assistant asked if she needed any help, June acted panicked, saying, 'No, no. Just looking around.' She really wanted to give the security guards something to say into their walkie-talkies, before she sailed out the door without having stolen (or bought) anything.

Of course, the security guards didn't need an excuse to talk into their walkie-talkies. That was what they were paid to do, and that was what they would do all day long, regardless of who came into or went out of the shop. It was their job.

But June didn't care about that. On her way to the bus stop, she was already imagining herself walking down a sunny street in Ratheane in cool new clothes, as people she knew said to themselves, 'There's June Corcoran. I'd love to look like her. She's so cool! I'd love to be like her.'

She was so wrapped up in this imaginary world that she almost missed the bus in the real world. She had to run to catch it as it pulled off. She needed a new bike, too. Where she would get the money for all these things was another day's work.

Turkey, Parrot, Pigeon

~

Pain pain pain! His shin was throbbing. He hopped into the bathroom. Everywhere he touched hurt, but then he realised he had a pain in his hand as well as one in his shin.

'Gerry, get that turkey out of the sink!'

'It's not a turkey, it's a pigeon.'

'Well, whatever it is, get it out of the sink!'

June's father Ben — short for Bernard, which is what his wife Gillian called him when they were having an argument — was a taxi-driver. He was also the manager of the local soccer team, which played on Saturdays. That afternoon something wonderful had happened. One of the players had been injured, and they had no sub to replace him, so Ben had had to go on. Ben was forty-seven (and a bit heavy in the belly), but this was his chance to show those young pups of twenty a thing or two. Like that lad running through with the ball, thinking he's Maradona. A good hard tackle and — 'Aaaaahhh! My leg! My leg!'

Ben's roars of pain had been so loud that the goalie's dog, who had been asleep behind the goal, woke up and bared his teeth in Ben's direction. Ben had limped around for the final two minutes; then, instead of changing in the dressing-room, he had driven straight home in his football gear as his shin turned forty shades of purple.

To find Gerry bathing this *bird* in the sink!

'I heard of people winning turkeys in raffles, but never a pigeon.'

'Supersonic is a racing pigeon, Dad. He's a very valuable bird.'

'How much did that raffle ticket cost you, son?'

'A pound,' said Gerry.

'You were robbed,' said Ben.

'No way. Uncle Jack is helping me train him. We're entering him in a race next weekend. If he wins, I get loadsamoney. And I'm sure he will win — won't you, Supersonic?' He kissed Supersonic on the head.

'Don't doo that,' said Supersonic in pigeon language. To Gerry, it just sounded like 'crroo-crroo'.

'Well, if Jack is on the case then I'm sure everything will be fine.' Ben was being sarcastic. Uncle Jack was Gillian's brother and, in Ben's words, 'a complete chancer'.

'Uncle Jack told me to give him a bath. Good for his feathers.'

'Save yourself the bother. Pluck him. Now out! Mind my *shin*!'

'Sorry.'

'And put the dinner on, your mother will be home soon.'

'Sure, Dad.'

'And close the door after you.'

Gerry closed the door and went downstairs to the kitchen. This suited Supersonic, who wasn't too keen on baths.

June had just arrived home and was getting a drink of Coke from the fridge. Supersonic said something which sounded like 'crroo-crroo' to Gerry — but June heard it as 'Coke, Coke!'

'I see that parrot hasn't flown away yet?' she said.

Gerry stood in the doorway, closed his eyes, took a deep breath and counted: one — two — three .... It was beginning to annoy him, the way people kept calling Supersonic a turkey, a parrot .... Only Gerry's mum had any time for him.

'He's a *pigeon*. A racing *pigeon*. A homing *pigeon*. And this is his home. He won't fly away.'

'Home,' said Supersonic, in his own language.

'Well, he perches on your shoulder like a parrot. Pigeons don't usually do that.'

This was true.

'He perches there 'cause he loves me. Don't you, Supersonic?' Gerry turned and kissed Supersonic on the beak, tickling him.

'Don't *doo* that!' said Supersonic.

'He hates you doing that,' June said.

'No he doesn't. Sure you don't, Supersonic?'

'I doo,' said Supersonic — or, as Gerry heard it, 'crroo'.

It was the first time Gerry had owned a bird (or any animal) and he was thrilled to have one this affectionate and clever. It didn't occur to him that he might be reading human qualities — even his own — into Supersonic's behaviour.

☆

June thought she was losing her mind.

She liked watching TV programmes about lions in Africa, and killer whales, but until recently she had thought birds were stupid and a waste of time. Two weeks before, when Gerry had brought Supersonic home after winning him in a raffle, her first reaction had been to raise her eyes to heaven. But as soon as she had done that, Supersonic had given her a look which seemed to say, 'What's the problem? This is my new home — get used to it.'

Often, by their behaviour, dogs and cats communicate to humans something of what's going on in their minds; but for birds it's quite rare. A pigeon in the park or a duck in a pond may indicate that it wants some of your sandwich — but that's about it.

June had looked again.

Not only did the pigeon's look seem to say, 'What's the problem? This is my new home — get used to it,' but the pigeon itself seemed to say these words. This bird with shiny green neck-feathers, a purple breast and pale blue wings was *talking* to her. The blood had drained from June's face.

Then she had laughed.

Ridiculous.

That's what happens when you don't get enough sleep at night. You start to have dreams — or nightmares — during the day. So June had just told Gerry, 'Great. Just what this house needs — a pet pigeon,' and stormed up to her room to try and get some sleep.

But she hadn't been tired. She hadn't been able to sleep.

And the next time she saw the pigeon, it had talked to her again!

June began to fear she was losing her mind. It was not as if she said, 'I think I'm going mad,' which most

people say from time to time but don't really mean —
it's just an expression of frustration or anger. June
really began to fear that she couldn't trust her mind to
tell her what was real and what was not real. And
when we can't trust our minds to tell us that, the world
becomes a very scary place.

She had panicked.

Then she calmed down; she told herself that, by some
freak of nature, she was so tuned in to the pigeon's
wavelength that she could understand what it was
thinking, and that it was no big deal. After all, she
could often tell what dogs and cats were thinking —
nothing very interesting, she reckoned, but she could
tell. That was it: she was just very sensitive to pigeons'
ways. Indeed, she was so sensitive to this pigeon's
ways that it was as if she could actually hear its voice.

But in the week following Supersonic's arrival,
something terrible and strange began to happen. The
cooing of pigeons in the street, the rattle of magpies in
the trees, the screeching of gulls overhead — all these
sounds, which until then had meant nothing to June,
she began to understand. It was like turning the dial of
a radio and hearing the crackle of static replaced by the
clear sounds of song and conversation. In the past
fortnight, all the birds in the world had seemed to June
to turn into parrots — not just parrots repeating the
same old 'Hello, give us a kiss' line, but parrots capable
of (relatively) intelligent conversation. It was because
of this that she had called Supersonic a parrot.

And yet it wasn't that she heard birds speak as she
heard humans speak. It was more like picking up
feelings which were so strong she understood them as
words. It was like those times in dreams when we hear
voices but no one is actually speaking.

June was seriously worried for her mind, but she

was afraid to talk to anyone, in case they confirmed what she feared most — that she was going mad.

There was one person whom she trusted, who might be able to help her. She had hoped to see him that morning. Shahin the fortune-teller knew about birds. His talisman was shaped like one.

☆

'Any chance of a drink of Coke there, June?' said Supersonic.

'No Coke for you.'

The horrible thing was that sometimes, without thinking, she talked back to the pigeon.

'I didn't ask for any,' Gerry said.

June thought quickly. 'Well — if you had — I wasn't going to give you any.'

Gerry stared at her. What was the story with June? 'I was getting some salted peanuts for Supersonic.'

'I've been eating salted peanuts all day. I'm parched. Get us a drink of Coke, ya big eejit!' In a bid to make Gerry understand, Supersonic turned and said this loudly into his ear.

'See,' said Gerry, flicking his fair hair off his forehead, 'he wants salted peanuts. Don't ya?' And he turned and kissed Supersonic on the beak.

Supersonic screeched and, in a flurry of feathers, flew over Gerry's head and onto his other shoulder.

'Gerry, he hates you doing that, and he wants a drink of Coke.'

'No he doesn't.'

'Yes I do. Coooke!' said Supersonic. He put so much effort into it that Gerry thought he really did hear 'Yes I do. Coke,' and not the normal gurgling 'crroo-crroo'.

He looked suspiciously at his sister.

'How come you always know what Supersonic says?'

'I don't. I just — guessed. Anyway, he's looking at my drink with his tongue hanging out. You don't have to be a mind-reader —'

'OK, OK,' said Gerry. He filled a saucer of Coke for Supersonic. 'Oh, by the way, Dad hurt his leg playing football.'

'What was he playing football for? He's too old to play football,' said June, angry not so much at her father as at herself for having talked to Supersonic.

'Well, don't tell him that. He hates being told he's too old,' said Gerry. Supersonic finished drinking, gave a satisfied pigeon burp and flew back to Gerry's shoulder. Gerry became very casual. 'Anyway, I'm off to Uncle Jack's to see about Supersonic's training. Mum will be home soon, so get the dinner. Bye.' And he made for the door.

'Gerry.'

He stopped and looked around. June was staring out the window and moving her tongue around in her cheek. The day had clouded since the bright morning, and it had started to drizzle.

'June?' Gerry said.

She watched the drizzle. She was thinking of Sian Whelan sitting down to a candlelit dinner with her loving, perfect (but sappy) parents. June's mother worked in a sandwich bar, and on Saturdays either June, Gerry or Ben had the dinner ready when she came home. It was their treat for her. Five times out of six, though, June ended up doing it. She was thinking of this, of being taken for granted, understood by no one (except that pigeon), unappreciated —

'June. What's wrong?' Gerry's voice intruded on her thoughts.

'Nothing's wrong.' June continued to stare at the rain, thinking of rollerblades and runners and bicycles

— thinking of anything other than her ability to communicate with birds.

'I know something's wrong,' said Gerry. 'Come on. You can tell me.' He spoke patiently, but, as usual, he was in a hurry to get to some place other than where he actually was — in this case, to Uncle Jack's.

'I'm depressed.'

'What about?' Gerry asked.

'I don't have cool rollerblades.'

That was it? 'But I don't have any rollerblades at all, and I'm not depressed.'

'And I don't have cool runners, or a new bicycle, or cool hair, or a new — a new — a new —'

'OK, OK,' said Gerry.

'I don't have a new anything, basically.'

'Well — that's life,' said Gerry, who seriously had to get going. 'Look, why don't you get the dinner and worry about this some other time?'

June looked at him coldly. 'You don't care.'

'I do.'

'You don't.'

Sometimes June had a way of leaning her head to the side and looking sadly at Gerry, as if she knew what he was thinking better than he knew himself. Gerry found this very irritating, and it often led to arguments. To keep calm, he counted to three again. 'I do care. It's just — all those things cost money.'

'You don't care. Nobody does. I'm having a — a personal crisis, and nobody cares. Might as well be talking to that pigeon.' She sneaked a glance at Gerry. He hadn't reacted to this. Could she tell him what was going on?

Gerry was thinking. 'I tell you what,' he said. 'If Supersonic wins the race next week, I'll buy you a pair of cool rollerblades. How about that?'

'Sure you will,' said June, not looking at him.

'And,' said Gerry reluctantly (he wanted to start saving up for a motorbike), 'I'll get you a pair of cool runners as well. How about that?'

'Do you mean it?' She turned towards him.

'Wouldn't say it otherwise.'

'You'll buy me stuff?'

'Whatever you want. I'll have loadsamoney when Supersonic starts winning races. He's probably the fastest racing pigeon in the country. That's what it said on the raffle ticket: "Tenth Prize, Supersonic — probably the fastest racing pigeon in the country."'

Already June was imagining the looks Sian Whelan would give her, and that made her forget her other problem. What problem? 'OK! Make sure and train him really hard. Every day. I'll help if you like.'

'What?' said Supersonic, and he burped again. 'Arrrp!' Gassy Coke.

'Don't worry about training. Uncle Jack will take care of that. You just get the dinner. Quick, before Mum gets in.'

And Gerry put on his leather jacket, ran out the door, and cycled to Uncle Jack's with Supersonic balancing on the handlebars of his bike. (This wasn't a trick Gerry had taught Supersonic. Incredibly, Supersonic did it of his own accord.)

Supersonic's Training

~

Uncle Jack was short and held his belly proudly in front of him, the way soldiers push their chests out on parade. His hair was dyed jet black and slicked back from his forehead, but his moustache was reddish brown. He was constantly on the verge of making 'serious money' and was always promising to bring June and Gerry to football matches, to the circus, or to the cinema. When the time came, he usually had something else to do, but he would promise faithfully to bring them 'next time'. He kept a flock of racing pigeons in a wooden loft in his back garden.

'No problem,' Uncle Jack had said on the phone, when Gerry told him about his pigeon; he'd 'train the bird'. Now it turned out he was going to be away, making deliveries in his van, and wouldn't actually be able to train Supersonic himself. Instead, he would give Gerry tips on pigeon-training and arrange to send

Supersonic to the release point.

In pigeon-racing, a special ring is put on each bird's leg; when the bird returns home, this ring is taken from its leg and used to stop a clock situated at a central clock station. The clock will have been running since the start of the race. In this way, the time it takes each bird to race home is measured. Uncle Jack would help Gerry get the clock and ring, but there was no way he could train Supersonic himself. Also, Supersonic would have to stay at Gerry's house, even though he seemed very much at home in Uncle Jack's loft and treated the other pigeons as old pals.

Uncle Jack told Gerry some things about racing pigeons. He said that they were descended from the wild rock-doves of the Mediterranean, and that the most important quality a racing pigeon could have was 'power orientation'. This was simply the ability to find its way home. Pigeons, Uncle Jack said, like to fly in flocks, where they will be protected from predators like the deadly peregrine falcon — possibly the fastest bird on earth, when it is diving, or stooping, on its prey. In any flock, there will be a small number of birds which are super-talented at finding their way home, and the others simply follow these natural leaders.

Jack didn't tell Gerry that he had once had a pigeon who was incredibly fast, with superb orientation — a natural leader, the most talented bird Jack had ever seen. But this bird, instead of flying straight home from training as he was supposed to, liked to hang out on street-corners eating the crisps and chips that people dropped on the footpath. Of course, the valuable racing pigeons would follow him off course and then be un-able to keep up when he suddenly flew swiftly away. Some, especially the younger birds, would get totally lost and not return home for days or weeks — if they got home at all!

In the end, Jack had decided that this bird was having such a bad influence on his flock that he would have to get rid of it. The question was, how? No one who knew anything about pigeons would buy it. By this stage, the bird was driving him so crazy he wanted to wring its neck; and he probably would have, had someone not asked him to donate a prize for a local raffle.

He had the solution. He let this pigeon be a prize in a raffle.

But first he put a tag on the bird's leg. The tag said, 'Supersonic — probably the fastest racing pigeon in the country.'

When his fourteen-year-old nephew Gerry told him he'd got a racing pigeon, Jack was delighted. Sure, he would help with the training! But when Gerry turned up with Supersonic, Jack stuck his belly out even further than usual and seemed to be trying to lick his moustache from his upper lip. That bird kept coming back to him like a boomerang! No. No way could he train with Jack's own pigeons. 'Much as I'd love to have him .... Better off training him yourself, Gerry. That's the way you'll learn.'

Jack gave Gerry some tips on the kind of mileage Supersonic should do each day, but he let Gerry himself carry out the plan.

☆

Supersonic was like someone who turns up for football without laces for his boots, or even without boots, but is brilliant once the game begins. Usually these are players who do what comes naturally to them and don't try to be like anyone else. But, no matter how much of a natural you are, you have to work and train. So it was with Supersonic.

In the week leading up to the race, Ben was doing the airport run with his taxi each morning. He would pick up passengers from their hotels and drive them to the airport; there he would pick up more passengers and drive them to their hotels in the city.

Gerry saw that the seventeen miles from the airport to their house would be a good training flight for Supersonic. Ben agreed, but added that he would rather carry a baby elephant to the airport than 'that dumb turkey'. June suggested putting Supersonic in the boot. Then Ben could release him at the airport. As Gerry would be at school, he could leave his bedroom window open, so Supersonic would be able to get in after flying home.

It was all arranged.

The only problem was Supersonic.

Unlike most birds, Supersonic liked to sleep late in the morning. And he did not like being put in the boot of a car.

On Monday morning, when he realised what was happening, he simply flew onto the roof of the house and refused to come down.

Gerry was in the garden, trying to sing Supersonic down: 'Super*sonic* .... Pleeese, *come* down ....'

Gillian, June and Gerry's mother, scattered imaginary grain in the garden and called, 'Tck-tck-tck,' as if she was feeding chickens.

June shouted, 'If you don't come down and train, I'll break your stupid useless neck.'

But Supersonic knew that if he didn't come down she wouldn't be able to do anything to him; and, anyway, he was too sure of Gerry's love for him to pay any heed to threats. He tucked his head under his wing and tried to go back to sleep.

Ben sat in the car with his head in his hands. If the neighbours wanted entertainment, well, the Corcorans would provide it. His whole family, in fact, would go out into the front garden at eight in the morning and try to persuade their one and only racing pigeon to fly down from the roof — whenever he woke up, of course.

It was then that June's ability to talk to Supersonic came in useful. Threats had had no effect on him — but what about bribes?

Casually, so no one would think she believed that Supersonic understood, she shouted that there would be a saucer of Coke and a bowl of peanuts in Gerry's room (where Supersonic slept at night) when he flew home from the airport. 'Now will you come down?'

June felt her face burning. This was the first time she had admitted to herself that she really was talking to Supersonic. Why not? It was worth it, if it would get him to train.

Sleepily, Supersonic brought his head out from under his wing. 'Say again, June?'

Casually, June repeated the bribe.

'Come on, Supersonic. Gerry will put Coke and peanuts in his room.' As far as the others were concerned, she might as well have been shouting, 'Come on, fetch the stick,' to a dog — or so she thought.

'Why dinja say that in the first place?' Casually, as if he was catching June's pretend mood, Supersonic yawned and launched himself off the roof, to float effortlessly down to the boot of the car. 'Away we go, boss! The airport,' he called to Ben, who was thinking of accidentally 'forgetting' to ever let Supersonic out. But no — no point in stinking up the car with a dead pigeon. Ben got out, slammed the boot shut, had a quick look around to see what neighbours were watching, and drove off to collect his first passengers.

Gerry was staring at June. He had noticed that Supersonic had responded to what she had said, but not to anyone else. There was something in the way she talked to Supersonic that was different from the way Gerry talked to him. What was it? It was the tone of her voice. It was a look in her eyes. It was everything. It was very strange.

No, it wasn't. It was the opposite of strange. It was natural. That was it: she was so easy and natural when she was talking to Supersonic. And for June, that *was* strange.

At least she had got him to come down from the roof. Soon he would be flying across the city, from the airport to the house — training for the race.

But Supersonic had great difficulty flying across a city without dropping down to see what was happening. Discipline was not a strong part of his nature. Each morning that week, Ben released him at the airport. And each morning Supersonic interrupted his flight home to hang out on street-corners, chatting to the ordinary street pigeons and eating crisps and chips. He particularly liked curry chips left over in cartons from the night before. Then he would play a trick on people: he would perch on a tree and relieve himself on someone passing underneath. His favourites were men with bald heads and schoolgirls with expensive hairstyles. He would then fly home at a blinding speed and demolish the peanuts and Coke in Gerry's room. He had the time of his life.

Gerry and June put his good spirits and liveliness down to increased fitness, and congratulated themselves on the training. They were sure they had a winner.

☆

June had a more difficult week. Sian Whelan's visit to the sports shop had been worse than she had thought. How could Mrs Whelan spend so much money on her? What was more, Sian announced — and announced, and announced — that her wonderful parents were taking her to EuroDisney in Paris, as a treat for her birthday, at the end of April. Sian was an only child, and her parents lavished all their attention on her — or, as June's father (and June) said, 'spoiled her like a pet cat'. The trip to Paris was making her seem even more glamorous, and everyone in the class wanted to be seen talking to her.

On Tuesday morning, June decided to tell everyone about her brother's new racing pigeon and the up-coming race.

There was a shocked silence from the girls in her group.

'A pigeon!'

'Yuk! Yuk*eeee*!'

Sian, her lustrous Queen-of-Sheba eyes almost popping out of her head, said, 'That's disgusting! You keep it in the *house*? Well, nothing that horrible brother of yours does would surprise me. Does he ever take that greasy leather jacket off?'

June felt herself blushing bright red. She hated it when her face betrayed her like that. It wasn't just the girls' reaction which embarrassed her. It was herself. She had honestly thought they would be impressed by her brother having a pigeon.

Over the last two days, she had found herself enjoying having Supersonic around. Maybe it was the involve-ment of helping to train him. She certainly got a thrill out of being able to understand him. It was this very thing which made her face burn now.

She was also embarrassed by what Sian had said about Gerry. June knew that her brother thought Sian was beautiful, and that he intended to ask her out when she grew up.

☆

Only Jennifer Adams disapproved of Sian Whelan going to EuroDisney. She thought it was a shocking waste of money, when there were so many poor people in the world. Only Jennifer didn't laugh at the thought of June's brother having a pigeon in the house. She didn't approve of pigeons, but, at the same time, she was June's friend.

Jennifer was regarded as the most boring girl in the class.

Her mother wore a ring in her nose and dyed her hair pink. She couldn't understand how her own daughter could be so sensible. (Jennifer's hair was a riot of red. For a while, when they'd been studying the Old Testament, she'd been nicknamed 'the Burning Bush'.)

Until recently, Jennifer had been a wild, crazy girl and a terrible practical joker. That time when she and June had gone to see Shahin, Jennifer had grabbed the talisman from the table and run off with it. She had been going to stuff it up the exhaust pipe of a bus. It had been her idea of a laugh.

But not Shahin's. June had caught Jennifer at the exit of the arcade and taken the talisman from her. She had never seen anyone as angry as Shahin had been when she gave it back to him. 'She has *interfered with my magic powers!*' he'd screamed, pulling at his shiny black hair. Only by holding the glittering statue in his brown fingers and muttering words in his own language had he been able to calm down.

'A terrible thing,' he'd said, when he was finally calm. 'Maybe one day this wrong will be righted and she will perform a brave deed in the service of another, as you have in returning my talisman. If not ....' He had shaken his head. 'Terrible thing.'

'Talk about overreaction,' Jennifer had said, when June told her about this. But that was the last smart-aleck comment June had ever heard her make. Since then, there had been no wildness and no practical jokes. Jennifer was completely sensible. In fact, she was more sensible than most of the teachers in school. She was almost — but not quite — a different person.

☆

As the day of the race drew near, June got more and more excited. She felt that the 'I want I want I want' voice was about to be answered, and that her life was about to change forever.

She didn't mention Supersonic at school again, and neither did she talk with him at home. She persuaded herself that she wasn't able to talk to birds, that it had all been a figment of her imagination. She did everything she could to help Gerry, because she was going to share in his winnings, but that was as far as it went. 'Birds are useless unless they're some use to you.' She wrote it in her notebook.

But on Friday something happened which made June write 'Most of the time,' before that sentence.

She was walking home from school with Jennifer, Sian and two other girls. They had just passed under a tree when Sian started shrieking like a scalded cat.

She was grabbing at her hair, which was covered in a smelly, slimy, silvery substance. She shivered and shrieked in disgust as it touched her fingers. 'My *hair*!' she screamed.

From the branches overhead came a flurry of rapidly flapping wings. A pigeon swooped over their heads and flew off. The pigeon had green neck-feathers, a purple breast and pale blue wings. It flew down the road towards June's house.

They calmed Sian down and brought her home.

That evening Supersonic got an extra saucer of Coke from June. She didn't speak, and neither did Supersonic, who was too busy slurping his drink. June told herself it was to give him energy.

Tomorrow was Saturday. The day of the race.

Racing North

~

All week, Winter, like a grey-bearded old warrior, had been battling with the young, fresh-faced Spring. On Tuesday afternoon, in a black fury, Winter had machine-gunned the country with hailstones, only for Spring to deftly whip the clouds away and breathe sunshiny breezes on the shivering land. If Winter sent clear, frosty nights, Spring responded with a thick blanket of cloud which kept the earth snug beneath it. On Friday night, under cover of darkness, Winter launched an ambush, hurling thunderbolts and lightning, rain, sleet and gales, in a desperate, destructive fury, until it seemed that nothing, not even Spring, could survive. By Saturday morning, you expected to find Winter triumphant, with a white snow-cloak and a frosty glare; but it was no-where to be seen. Maybe it lay tangled, exhausted, in the broken old ash tree by the roadside, which was the sole evidence of its efforts in the night.

Meanwhile there was Spring — calm, unruffled, whistling along to the tune of a thousand birds. He seemed to say, 'Look, Nature. I've provided the conditions: a cloudless blue sky, bright sunshine. Now come on, leaves — start budding, buddies! Grow, grass, grow! Flowers, let's be having you! Don't worry about that old Winter. I've kicked his ass.'

☆

At eight in the morning, five hundred pigeons were loaded into a truck with compartments that allowed the racers to be released within moments of one another. It was a race for young birds, the first of the year, and the pigeons were tremendously excited. They stood, heads up, chests out, talking non-stop about their own lofts to birds from other lofts, and about the race to come with their own companions. Most competing lofts had sent a number of birds, but of course Gerry could only enter Supersonic.

On the drive through the countryside, there was much talk about who would win the race. Some pigeons were modest about their own chances, but others cockily predicted success for themselves and sang out their racing-calls like boxers boasting before a fight. Of these, the most arrogant and confident was a haughty blue-grey bird with fiery orange eyes. Banishing all debate, he sang out steadily and with dramatic self-importance:

'I am Lionel the First.

Forget about the rest.

See my flaming orange eyes.

You are looking at the best!'

He gazed around imperiously. It takes guts to really believe you're better than anyone else, and it was obvious that Lionel the First had absolutely no doubts about his right to regard himself as the best.

The thing about pigeons' racing-calls is that they must be sung with utter conviction. When rival gorillas meet in the jungle, they beat their chests aggressively, and the one who gives the least impressive display is the one who must give way — they rarely actually fight. In the same way, pigeons themselves would happily do without racing and judge one another solely on the strength of their racing-calls. Make no mistake: nervous bluffing carries no weight in the pigeon world. What counts with racing-calls is steely self-belief, the ability to nervelessly stare down and out-call your opponent.

The other pigeons looked at Lionel the First, cocking their heads as pigeons do because their eyes are on the sides.

'Was that the first or the last?' a voice called out. 'Did he say he was the first or the last, or the least, or what?'

(It should be pointed out here that the pigeons were not using these actual words. These are the words they would have used if they had been speaking English instead of pigeon. You could call this a kind of pigeon English.)

'And who might you be, sir?' asked Lionel the First, putting as much mockery into the 'sir' as pigeon language allows — and pigeon language allows for an awful lot of mockery.

All eyes turned to the upstart pigeon; but he didn't wilt under the attention. Instead he started to bop his head up and down and hop from side to side, rapping out in a husky voice:

'I am Supersonic,
So you be realistic.
I look like I'm a rocket,
And I fly like I'm ballistic!'

The other pigeons were stunned. This call had the authority of a gunshot, and it was just as impossible to argue with. Supersonic had sung tunelessly, but with a no-holds-barred, slightly crazy energy. There wasn't the slightest chink of self-doubt, of nerves.

In the ritual of racing-calls, the honour goes to the pigeon who is asked to repeat its call. Supersonic stood, steely-eyed, daring the racers to even consider anyone else. There was a tense silence.

Then, without any discussion among themselves, as if by magic, all the pigeons decided at the same instant who should be awarded the honour. To Lionel the First's speechless fury, they asked Supersonic to repeat his call. This he did, again and again, and each time there was a murmur of appreciation from 498 of the other 499 birds.

Then the time came to sing 'The Dance', an ancient pigeon song which all young pigeons learn in the loft.

Supersonic's parents had tried to teach it to him when he was a chick, but he hadn't been too interested in learning ancient pigeon songs, and he still wasn't. Anyway, something about this song made him feel very uneasy.

Instead, he gave yet another rendition of 'I am Supersonic', and this prevented the singing of 'The Dance'. A very young bird called Jimmybuckle tried to start a chorus of the pigeon version of 'Stop the Bus, We Want a Wee-Wee', but he didn't get very far. Meanwhile, Lionel the First had started to repeat his own call, partly in defiance of Supersonic and partly to convince himself that he was Supersonic's equal. This did have the effect of giving others the courage to get in on the act, but many of their calls carried little conviction. For example:

'I am Jimmybuckle.

I fly very fast.

I have brown wings and feathers.'

(Long long pause for thought.)

'I hope I won't be last.'

Order had broken down. It had dawned on the pigeons that they would really have to race, and that being awestruck by Supersonic or Lionel the First might not be enough to get them safely home. To give themselves a boost, they sang out their racing-calls. The truck was a riot of confusion.

The driver couldn't understand why the pigeons were making such a racket in the back. He wished they'd stop. The cooing sounds, and having had to get up so early, were making him sleepy.

After a long drive down the busy Saturday-morning roads, the truck arrived at Carnsore Point, in the southeast corner of Ireland, and the driver gratefully released the birds.

They exploded into the clear air. It was as if a bag of feathers had been emptied in front of a powerful electric fan — *whooooshhh*!

Then there was the loud leathery slapping of a thousand flapping wings as the pigeons circled the truck to get their bearings.

'The sun's blinding me.'

'Outta my way.'

'Don't fly to the sun. That's east. We're going north.'

'North? Yeah, I *know* — Which way is —'

'North's this way, idiot.'

'It's this way!'

'No, that way.'

'Not that way, this way.'

'Not this way, that way.'

'Which way?'

'This way.'

'Dublin?'

'Dublin? This way.'

'This way!'

Whooooshhh!

Off they flew.

☆

If you are lost and need to get somewhere, there are two things you need to find out. The first is which directions are north, south, east, and west. This is called 'compass'. The second thing is where you are in relation to where you want to go. This is called 'map'. Not knowing where you are, but knowing which direction to take, is not as bad as not knowing where you are *and* not knowing which direction to take.

People think homing pigeons have an inbuilt sense of compass and map. It's thought they can find out where north, south, east and west are from the positions of the sun, moon and stars. It's also thought that they can sense the earth's magnetic field, which is strongest at the North and South Poles and weakest at the Equator. They may also use sound and smell. No one knows how they get their sense of map — how they know if they are north, south, east or west of where they want to go. But they do know.

Less scientific people think pigeons can tune in to the wavelengths coming from their own homes and fly towards them as simply as moths flying towards a light.

Pigeons themselves aren't bothered about how they do it. They just do it. In fifteen seconds they were shooting north, at almost fifty miles an hour, in the direction of Dublin. And the two pigeons at the head of the flock were Lionel the First and Supersonic.

Despite having lost the battle of the calls, Lionel the First was determined to show that he was superior to these chickens who thought themselves racing pigeons. Supersonic was driven by sheer panic. *What was this —* this green stuff?

'What's the story?' he shouted, as they flew over the green countryside.

'Grass,' shouted the other pigeons.

Grass!

Of course Supersonic had seen grass before, but never this much of it. Who needs all this grass?!

'And what are those monsters down there going "Moooo"?' he shouted.

'Cows,' shouted some pigeons who had been in the countryside before.

Cows? Mad-looking yokes. 'And those vicious white things going "Maahahaha" — what are they? Some kind of giant cats?'

'Sheep,' shouted the pigeons at the back, and they told Supersonic they were harmless.

Supersonic wasn't so sure. His wings beat faster and faster. Lionel the First was straining just to stay abreast. Many of the slower pigeons were being left behind by Supersonic's incredible speed.

Lionel the First was getting worried because, while he was definitely racing Supersonic, Supersonic seemed unconcerned about him. He was scornful of Supersonic's ignorance about cattle and sheep and grass — unbelievable! He was a bit jealous, though, of the way Supersonic didn't care what other pigeons thought of him. If Lionel the First didn't know what something was, he never said so, in case someone laughed at him.

On his right he saw Supersonic edge ahead. This was unbelievable! How much faster could he go? Lionel the First increased his speed, wondering how much longer he could keep this up.

A truly horrible sight had prompted Supersonic's latest acceleration. Below them, the land had gone completely black.

'What's happening?' he shouted. 'Have they burnt the place?'

'No, they ploughed it,' shouted the other pigeons. 'Slow down.'

But Supersonic didn't slow down — because the black land and the green land and, way off to their right, the blue sea, were patrolled by hundreds, thousands, of birds. Gulls, crows, rooks, starlings, ducks — *whish*! Oh, man, do ducks fly fast! You'd never think it, to see them on the ground .... Then there were what sounded like millions of birds, whom Supersonic couldn't see but could hear, holding a song contest in the bushes ....

Supersonic had seen other birds before — the odd gull on a goalpost or swan in a pond. But he had thought the world was run by pigeons, people, and those huge coloured beetles that kept swallowing people up and spitting them out again — the things Gerry called 'heynicewheelsman' or 'heycoolsexymotor' and June called 'cars'. It was a big shock to his system to find that there were so many other birds in the world.

More green. More black. More *birds*.

Where were the streets? The buildings? The smoke? The fumes? Everything Supersonic knew and loved? Faster and faster he flew, in a desperate bid to get home — which is where a homing pigeon is happiest.

The sun climbed higher above the sea in the east. As in athletics races, smaller groups began to break off the back of the flock and fall further and further behind the leaders. On and on they flew, over miles and miles of countryside. There were times during the morning when Supersonic's heart gave a joyful leap at the sight of buildings, but then he'd see that these weren't Dublin, and he would fly on.

Once, his curiosity got the better of him. Instead of flying over the town, he swooped down, followed by the fifteen other pigeons who had somehow managed to keep pace with him.

When Supersonic began his descent, Lionel the First thought about flying on alone, but he was too exhausted. He went down with the others, intending to have a nice rest, find a bite to eat, and then sneak off when they weren't looking.

The town was Arklow. Nice place, Supersonic thought. Bit small and slow for his taste, but nice. The old ladies weren't too quick about chucking bits of bread to the visiting pigeons, but there were plenty of chips and half-eaten burgers lying around. There were a few too many jackdaws with attitude problems, but no matter. The local pigeons weren't a bad lot, and of course they were hugely impressed by their visitors from the city.

In fact, Supersonic was getting some of his old confidence back. 'Outta me way!' he shouted, and a local pigeon stepped smartly aside to let him have the chip. See? Easy! What had he been so worried about? 'Shoo!' he said, and another local pigeon let Supersonic stick his beak into an upturned Pepsi can. 'Glug, glug ....' The Pepsi was about three days old, just the way Supersonic liked it. Ahh, the countryside! You can't beat it. Now — how about getting home?

Supersonic took off like a shot from a catapult. He was a dot on the horizon before the others realised what was happening.

Lionel the First, taking a breather on a car bonnet, was caught by surprise. That was what *he* had intended to do! He couldn't believe it.

But he still intended to win. Most pigeons would have given up, but Lionel the First was a very strong character. With a painful effort, he stretched his tired wings and propelled himself into the air. All the other racing pigeons followed.

Well, all but one. One racer with brown wing-feathers was listening, enthralled, to a local bird's description of the biggest treat known to pigeon — finding a kebab wrapper with some leftover kebab in it. Oh, boy! Enough to make a pigeon drool at the beak .... He looked around for a kebab wrapper, but there was nothing to be seen. In fact — where, ah — where were the, ah — the, ah — the other racers?

'Anyone see ...? — Gone? *Gone!* Where? Which way? Which —'

Young Jimmybuckle was suddenly very frightened. His orientation, his sense of direction, wasn't the best. He did have an inbuilt sense of compass and map, like all homing pigeons, but he never used them. He was one of those pigeons who are happy to stay at the back of the group and let others take the lead. When it came to finding his own way and thinking for himself, he wasn't too comfortable. But that was exactly what he would have to do if he was going to get home.

He said a quick farewell to the Arklow pigeon and took off.

The Dance

~

Supersonic was happy. He always got a kick out of that trick of leaving the other pigeons behind. With every beat of his wings he was getting closer to home. He had latched on to a warm breeze, which felt cool as he rocketed through it.

Boooom!

Gone.

That was him. Don't blink or you'll miss —

Blinked. Missed him.

☆

He was flying along the coast. He came to an inlet where the rocky land loomed hundreds of feet above his head on his left, and sloped to the sea hundreds of feet below him to the right. He didn't take the shortest route and fly straight over the water; instead he kept to the arc of the inlet, avoiding the strong crosswinds out to sea. He was doing everything that a good racing pigeon should, leading the race and getting closer to winning the prize money for Gerry and June. Not that that was of any importance to Supersonic. All that mattered to him was getting home.

If he'd had the time, he would have gone and done a spot of yodelling with those birds on the ground. They thought they were happy! He'd show them what happiness was. Ah, the countryside! The sea! The sun! The spring — when a young bird's fancy turns to fun .... Adjusting his position slightly so as to stay on course, he thought he saw a shadow detach itself from the sun. He tried to make up a song to reflect his happy mood:

'If you need a tonic
Send for Supersonic.
Biff, boom, bing —
Pigeon on the wing!'

Something caught his eye, and his heart gave one of those involuntary leaps of joy it had given whenever he thought he saw Dublin on the horizon. But this time he really did see something familiar. Amazingly, out here in the countryside — a crisp bag! Even though he wasn't too hungry, after his recent snack, Supersonic couldn't help but look.

Far down below, three people were having a picnic. They had crisps ... and something that looked like a big bottle of .... One of the people, a girl, drank from this bottle .... It was that delicious drink that Gerry called 'sevenhup'.

Just watching the girl drink made Supersonic thirsty. He veered from his flight path, losing altitude to get a closer look. He recognised the girl. Yes, there was no mistake. He had played a trick on that girl yester —

Then a shadow swung out of the sun like a ball on an invisible chain and exploded by the side of his head.

Supersonic went tumbling earthwards, head over tail. He felt a hot pain in his right wing. Something had narrowly missed his head and struck his wing. He somersaulted, as much to dodge what had attacked him as from loss of control. One part of his mind told him that watching the picnic had exposed him to danger, and that veering from his flight path had saved him. Another, more urgent part of his mind told him that the danger was still present.

He pulled out of his fall and looked around. He saw nothing. It seemed he was alone in the sky, but he knew this was not the case.

Panic was beginning to lock his wings when he remembered something his parents had taught him when he was a chick. He instantly dipped to the left.

It saved his life.

This time the bomb struck from below, but Supersonic wasn't there. He remembered what his parents had told him: peregrine falcons usually attack your blind spot — they come out of the sun, or from below. And he was being attacked by a peregrine falcon. On its dive, or stoop, it is one of the fastest living things on earth.

The falcon was above him and to his left, only a room's length away. Supersonic recognised, as any pigeon would, the sickle-shaped silhouette, the long pointed wings, the hooked beak and the big eyes which, unlike a pigeon's, stare straight ahead. Those eyes were watching him very calmly. There was no hatred or anger in them — and no mercy.

Supersonic was a pigeon with a naturally high opinion of himself. He was adored by Gerry, he was popular with other pigeons, and he had no trouble

ignoring people like Uncle Jack when they were annoyed with him. It was quite a shock to him to share the sky with a bird to whom all this counted for nothing, a bird whose piercing eyes calmly regarded him as dinner — nothing more, nothing less.

The falcon was still away to the left, but she was gaining on Supersonic by the split second. She (female falcons are larger than males — this was a female) could scythe through the air at a speed impossible to follow with the naked eye. But Supersonic had the edge in manoeuvring — twisting and turning in small spaces. Just as the falcon was about to strike, Supersonic changed direction, and for the third time the falcon overshot her mark.

Supersonic knew he was trapped in the inlet. It was like being in one half of a giant football stadium, with the sea on the other side. If he could escape the great walls looming above him, he might reach freedom.

He climbed upwards, higher and higher, his lungs and wings straining. Out of the corner of his eye he saw the falcon zooming in, like an arrow towards its target. Without hope of success, he flicked to the right. Mercifully, she missed. Higher. The walls blurred with his speed.

He burst clear of the inlet and saw the spring country-side rolling away in the distance. He swooped towards it, in a desperate bid for freedom. Yes! He'd esca —

To his horror, the falcon appeared in front of him, blocking his path. Having been fooled four times, she was now beginning to second-guess Supersonic: instead of striking where he was, she was aiming for where she thought he would dodge. Like a sheepdog herding a sheep, she turned him back down into the inlet, away from the countryside he might never see again.

As the falcon coolly watched, preparing her strike,

Supersonic hurtled towards the sea. The song his parents had tried to teach him when he was a chick, the song he had refused to listen to on the truck, came back to haunt him:

The Dance

Pirouette on the evening breeze;
Dip to the left, spin — one two three —
Swooping low over fields of clover,
And around the sycamore tree.
If you go right then I am free ....

No rest till the dance is over.
Winged death follows me.

Supersonic and the falcon swooped and looped downwards, in a dance which you will see on no stage or ballroom — a twisting, turning, curving dance of death.

Picnic by the Sea

~

On this particular Saturday afternoon, Sian Whelan had gone for a drive down by the coast with her mum and dad. They parked their car on the coast road and had a picnic overlooking the sea. They were in an inlet whose walls, half cliff, half mountain, sloped high above their heads. Below them was a railway line, and they watched a train emerge from a tunnel on its way from Wexford to Dublin. Below that, the sparkling sea lapped at the sharp rocks where huge black seabirds basked. The air was clear as crystal. Mr and Mrs Whelan held hands and looked dreamily out to sea.

'It's lovely,' said Mrs Whelan.

'Isn't it,' said her husband.

'Absolutely beautiful,' said Mrs Whelan.

'The air is as sweet as — as —' Mr Whelan couldn't think what the air was as sweet as, so he said, 'It's so peaceful and calm and so — lovely.'

They squeezed each other's hand and gazed at the waves. They were having a beautiful moment, with their daughter by their side.

But their daughter was not looking out to sea. She was staring in the other direction, up at the walls of the inlet.

One pigeon looked much the same as another to Sian, but that pigeon flying overhead seemed very much like the one that had attacked her yesterday. She had her suspicions that the pigeon which had attacked her — done that disgusting thing on her head — was greasy-leather-jacket Gerry Corcoran's pigeon. But what was it doing down here?

Could this be the race June had mentioned? Sian was trying to remember what June had said about the race when, suddenly, the most shocking thing she had ever seen happened.

Something struck the pigeon from above, and it disappeared.

That was all Sian saw, but she instantly began to replay it in her mind, and it seemed to her that she had seen an awful lot more. It seemed that she had seen the pigeon flying along and then seen another bird dive on it from an enormous height, with its wings closed. The other bird hadn't just been falling; it had seemed to be propelled earthwards like a lightning bolt. It had hit the pigeon on the head with a solid *thunk*. (Sian hadn't heard the *thunk*, but her imagination supplied it.) The pigeon had fallen out of the sky, followed by the other bird, which had swooped, snatched the pigeon in its talons and flown off with it towards the cliff-face, where it had disappeared.

All this had happened in about three seconds, or so it seemed.

Sian looked at her parents. They were still gazing

out at the sea, talking about how lovely it was. She couldn't tell them that the most violent thing she had ever witnessed had just happened above their heads. Or had she imagined it?

Yes?

No?

Maybe?

No. She had seen it. And she would not spoil her parents' dreamy mood by telling them about it.

A nasty grin appeared on her beautiful face. She would tell June Corcoran instead.

The Race of No Return

~

'Well, Gerry, not to worry — at least one of us has won a prize! I can be so lucky — lucky, lucky, lucky .... What am I saying?' said Ben. 'Luck had nothing to do with it. Pure skill, that was!'

The prize Ben was talking about was a week's holiday for two in a castle hotel in the West of Ireland. The President of the United States had once stayed there. Film stars and prime ministers stayed there. And the next week, Ben and Gillian would be staying there. Ben had won this prize on a radio phone-in competition. Contestants had had to imitate a horse neighing. (The hotel was famous for its horse-riding facilities.) Ben's horse imitation was startlingly good (he was better at imitating a horse than at riding one), and he had won the competition.

'Still,' he continued, 'I'm sure that pigeon will get back soon.'

'Ben,' said Gillian in a warning voice.

'Let's see,' said Ben, ignoring her. 'This is Tuesday evening. He should have been back on Saturday —'

'Ben, leave him alone,' said Gillian.

'It is a long way from Wexford to Dublin. But it's not *that* long. Unless, of course, he's not a pigeon at all. You know, son, he did look very like a turkey to me.'

'*Bernard*!' Gerry's mother was slim, with clear skin and very bright eyes — which she got, Ben said, from her ability to see only what was good in people. She was sitting beside Ben on the sofa, with her legs curled up beneath her. In her right hand she held a rolled-up magazine like it was a stumpy baseball bat.

Ben shut up.

It was eight o'clock in the evening, and they were in the living-room. June had gone up to her bedroom. Three days had passed since the race, but there was no sign of Supersonic. Uncle Jack had been in, earlier that evening, and had told Gerry that 'these things happen'. Apparently Supersonic wasn't the only pigeon that hadn't come back. In fact, Uncle Jack had seemed surprised that *any* of the pigeons had returned.

He had come over to see Gillian, his sister. She wanted him to look after Gerry and June while she and Ben were away at the hotel. Gerry and June had been indignant. They were old enough to be left at home alone — thanks very much for your concern, but no need to worry.

Uncle Jack had agreed. 'Big chap like Gerry — well able to look after himself. Well able. Tha' right, Gerry? I'm going to be busy with the van next week. Lotta deliveries. Very busy.' Uncle Jack had sucked on his reddish-brown moustache and smoothed back his hair (which he dyed black, to make himself look like Elvis Presley). He had seemed to be thinking of something. 'I might drop over in the evenings, though. Just to make sure they're eating properly.'

'Oh, that would be great,' Gillian had said. She was very fond of her brother. She had told Gerry and June that he had always been a bit wild, like a lot of fellas, but he had a good heart. Ben and June were not so forgiving.

Uncle Jack had said, 'I hear young June's not a bad cook. I might call over around six in the evenings — that's when you have your dinner, yeah? Make sure they're getting the proper vitamins.'

'You're awful good, Jack,' Gillian had said, and she'd asked him if he'd like to have something to eat then.

'No no no no. No need to bother about me,' he'd said.

'We're having something ourselves,' Gillian had said.

'Well, if that's the case, I'll have whatever you're having.' June thought that Uncle Jack had a way of getting people to do things for him without asking. Gerry didn't think he meant any harm, but it drove June mad. She had shot him an angry stare which he hadn't seemed to notice. Their mother had gone to the kitchen to prepare a meal.

For three days Gerry had been inspecting the southern sky with the hopefulness and helplessness of someone waiting for a late bus. At first he thought every bird would turn out to be Supersonic. By Tuesday, he was able to rule them out while they were still dots on the horizon.

'But what could have happened to him?' he had asked Uncle Jack.

'Bad weather might have blown him off course.'

'Saturday was the nicest day of the year.'

'Was it?' Uncle Jack had tried to remember Saturday. 'Then maybe he got to like it down in the countryside. Maybe he doesn't want to come home.'

'Course he wants to come home. He's a homing pigeon. He loves it here.'

'Well, then, let's see — what else could have happened to him?' Uncle Jack had thought for a few seconds. 'Maybe a peregrine falcon got him,' he'd said.

'A what?'

'I told you before about peregrine falcons. A great menace to the racing pigeon.'

'Why? What do they do?' June had asked.

Jack had told her that they wait up in the sky, up to a mile above the earth, and when they see a duck or a pigeon passing underneath (their vision is eight times sharper than a human's, he said) they fold back their wings and dive on their prey. He said these stoops can reach speeds of a hundred and fifty miles an hour. Out of nowhere, the falcon hits the duck or gull or pigeon with its talons and kills it. To drive home this point, Jack had brought his pudgy hands together with a mighty *thunk*! 'Stone cold dead,' he'd said. 'End of story and good night. Over and out. The end.' And as if that wasn't bad enough, he had told them that sometimes falcons pluck their prey in mid-air — 'no bother to them' — before eating it.

June had listened with her mouth open.

Gerry had tried not to listen. The thought of that happening to Supersonic sickened him. It couldn't happen. Supersonic was too smart.

Uncle Jack had enjoyed the shocked response. He had gone on to tell them that certain people were prepared to pay big money for falcons. Princes in Arabia used them for falconry. It was totally illegal to take birds of prey from the wild, but Uncle Jack knew someone with contacts in the shipping business who was willing to take the risk. (Uncle Jack had contacts everywhere — all of them great risk-takers.)

Even now, an hour after Uncle Jack had left, Gerry was still trying to banish from his mind the *thunk* sound Jack's hands had made. It wasn't easy. He left his mother and father in the living-room and went to his bedroom.

'Happy now you've upset him?' Gillian asked Ben.

'Upset him? What did I do to upset him? He's only lost a pigeon. Sure, there's thousands more out in the street.'

Gillian shook her head. Gerry was sensitive and caring, like her — something Ben, for all his good nature, would never understand.

☆

It was early April, and the young Spring was wearing, in contrast to his usual sunny expression, a cold, severe face. Wind bent the bushes in the back garden and rattled the window in Gerry's room. He switched on the heater and strummed his guitar.

June came in. She looked worried. She said she had something to tell him.

'What?' Gerry asked.

June sat on the bed. Darkness shrouded the small room, so she switched on the bedside lamp. She flicked her long black hair away from her face. She didn't seem to want to say whatever was on her mind.

'What do you have to tell me?' Gerry asked.

'Sian Whelan was in Wicklow on Saturday, and she saw a pigeon being killed by a peregrine falcon.'

'How would Sian Whelan know what a peregrine falcon was?'

'She doesn't. But it sounded like one, from what Uncle Jack said. That's exactly what she saw.'

'So? A peregrine falcon attacked a pigeon in Wicklow on Saturday. It wasn't Supersonic.'

June hated having to say this. In fact, it had been yesterday — Monday — when Sian Whelan had told June what she'd seen. First thing in the morning at school — 'Justice has been done!' she'd exclaimed. 'The pigeon that attacked me is *dead*!'

'Gerry, Sian said it was Supersonic. Remember, she knows what he looks like. She saw him on Friday.'

June had told Gerry what Supersonic had done to Sian. She had also told him what Sian had said about pigeons, and as a result Gerry was now less besotted with Sian. (June hadn't told him what Sian had said about him and his leather jacket. She'd thought, correctly, that he would be more likely to turn against Sian for insulting pigeons than for insulting him.)

'She doesn't know him well enough to recognise him. I'm telling you, Supersonic is too smart to get killed by a falcon. He's probably the fastest racing pigeon in the country.'

'But peregrine falcons are probably the fastest birds in the world!' said June.

'I don't care what they are. Supersonic is alive.'

June felt sorry for him — for being such a softie, for getting so attached to things. She knew he was afraid to admit to himself that Supersonic was dead. That was the thing about getting fond of birds or animals: they just caused you grief.

She lay on the bed, in the warm glow of the bedside lamp, and listened to Gerry strumming his guitar. He had a lovely dreamy style. He sat on the floor with his back to the bed, moodily looking out of the darkening window as he played.

Even June felt a little sad that she would never see Supersonic again. She was prepared to forgive him for not winning any money, if only he would come back.

Earlier, in her own room, she had written in her

notebook, 'Often things don't work out the way you want them to.' Now she thought she should have written, 'Often things never work out the way you want them.' But that was bad grammar. 'Things never work out the way you want them to,' she should have written.

She tried to think of a time when things had worked out exactly the way she had wanted them to. There had been times, but June couldn't remember them clearly. She couldn't remember anything clearly, because she was falling asleep listening to Gerry's dreamy guitar-playing and the wind whistling through the bushes in the back garden.

The Monster of the Cave

~

On that terrible final dive, Supersonic had begun to accept death as his fate. There was a hot pain in his wing, his breast muscles hurt and his lungs begged him to give up and be eaten. It was as if there was an actual voice saying that giving up would be easier than fighting. The pain would be over in a second, and then he would have a nice long long long rest ....

But another voice said, 'No. *Fight*! Fight until your last breath and heartbeat!'

The result of these two voices was that, as the falcon struck for the last time, Supersonic folded his wings and dropped like a stone to earth.

Whether he intended to or not, the important thing was that he dropped a split second before the falcon struck. The falcon didn't touch him. The rocks by the coastline rushed towards him, and they were just yards away when Supersonic spread his wings and floated.

To his left he saw the black mouth of a cave, and with one wingbeat he slipped into its darkness. He waited.

And waited.

☆

In the sky above, the falcon watched. She saw the pigeon go into the hole, but she didn't see him come out again. If he did come out, she would see him.

She began to circle and climb, her eyes scanning the ground for movement. Nothing came from the hole. She would not fly into its darkness, where her powerful vision would be useless.

She climbed higher and looked over the horizon. She could see for miles in the clear air. Far below, she saw three humans: a he-human and a she-human looking out at the water, and a smaller she-human looking at the sky.

The falcon's crop was hollow and cold. She would have to eat soon or endure a night of hunger. There was no movement from the hole in the ground.

She climbed higher, and more territory came into view. Far away to the south, she saw another group of pigeons flying in her direction. Still higher she rose, watching all the time.

One pigeon was flying ahead of the others. She held it in her sights until she was in a direct line between the sun above and the pigeon far below. So tenderly did she watch the pigeon that part of her was feeling the pigeon's unawareness of being watched. Being a true hunter, she had almost become her prey.

Of their own accord, the falcon's wings folded, and her unearthly wind-whistling stoop began. This time hunger made her strike keen and accurate and clean. She killed the pigeon with one blow to the head, snatched it in her talons and flew with it to a plucking post. When it was plucked, she brought it to her eyrie and ripped hungrily at the warm, bloody flesh.

There was a ring on the pigeon's leg, and on it were printed words the falcon could not read. The words were 'Lionel the First'.

☆

Far inside the cave, it was pitch black. What a long cave! How long were caves? Did they go on forever? Supersonic didn't know.

He did know he was in no hurry to go out again. And as for going up in the air — thanks, but no thanks. As long as that flying bomb was in the sky, Supersonic would give it a miss.

So this was the nice peaceful countryside? This was a place to relax? You must be joking! All day, Supersonic had been of the opinion that he could take or leave the countryside, but now he knew that he definitely wanted to leave it. The question was, how?

He couldn't think of a way. He perched on a stone by the cave wall and looked into the blank darkness.

Then the cave began to rumble and shake.

First it was just a gentle shake and a nice low rumble. It was quite pleasant. Then it got louder and shakier, until the cave hummed and rocked itself into a deafening, high-pitched scream, and a white light rushed towards Supersonic out of the blackness.

Oh no! Here she came again. When they wanted to get you, they were deadly serious about it. Supersonic's parents had never told him that falcons had these powers. This time there was no escape. The light zapped him, shook him, screamed in his ears and rattled his bones. On and on it went, higher and higher, piercing his blood, his marrow, for ever and ever, lower and lower and lower ....

And then — silence. Silence and darkness.

Was he dead? He still had a pain in his wing, he was hungry, and he wanted a drink of Coke. If this was death, it was very like life had been for the past few minutes, and Supersonic didn't like it.

He crouched on his stone and waited — and waited. For a long time — he didn't know how long — there was nothing but blackness and silence. It seemed that blackness and silence was all there ever had been and all there ever would be.

Then the screaming white cave-monster came once more. Once more Supersonic was shaken and zapped to lunacy and back; but again the monster refrained from eating him.

More blackness and silence.

Oh, man!

Supersonic's worst nightmares — when he dreamed of being lost (terrifying for a homing pigeon), or of clean streets with no overflowing rubbish-bins — had not prepared him for this. Could this be pigeon hell, like Gerry's father was in human hell when he watched the thing called 'theponies' on the thing called 'theTV'?

Supersonic heard a noise in the mouth of the cave. It sounded like — footsteps. Pigeon footsteps. Then he heard a voice, and it was definitely a pigeon voice. It was saying .... What was it saying?

Supersonic listened intently. Some sort of country accent? 'I'm lost. I'm lost,' said the voice.

How could he be lost if he was a country pigeon? This was the countryside.

The voice was high-pitched, timid and young-sounding: 'I'm lost, I'm lost, I'm lost, I'm last ....'

I'm *last*! It wasn't a country pigeon saying 'I'm lost'; it was a city pigeon saying 'I'm last'.

'Hey! Who's there?' said Supersonic.

Silence.

'Speak, or have your gizzard ripped asunder and fed to the maggots of the bright blue yonder. Speak, why don't you, or you will die; your blood will stiffen and your bones will dry.'

The last thing Supersonic wanted was a fight, so he had to make his threat as serious-sounding as possible. If your threat is threatening enough, you rarely need to back it up with action.

Silence.

The sound of a throat being meekly cleared.

'I am Jimmybuckle.

I fly very fast.

I have brown wings and feathers.'

(A sad resigned sigh.)

'I think that I am last.'

The other pigeon scuffled the stones with his feet and sighed again.

'*Jimmybuckle!*'

Supersonic had never in his life been so glad to meet another pigeon. He rushed to Jimmybuckle, and they felt for each other's beak in the darkness and rubbed them together in greeting. 'How did you get here?'

Jimmybuckle told Supersonic how he had been left behind in Arklow when the other pigeons flew off. At first he hadn't known which direction Dublin was in, but then he had seen the train. He'd remembered seeing a train in Dublin, so he had thought that all he needed to do was follow it and he would get home.

'Very good, Jimmybuckle. Good thinking,' said Supersonic. He couldn't believe Jimmybuckle had such bad directional sense that he needed to follow a train, but he didn't say anything. Already he was feeling more confident, now that he was with a younger pigeon who needed looking after.

'But the train went too fast for me. "Goodbye, train, I hope I see you again sometime," I said. So I followed the road that followed the train that —'

'Tracks. They're tracks, Jimmybuckle, not a road,' said Supersonic.

'I followed the tracks. I followed the tracks and I followed the tracks and I followed the tracks. And the sun went to sleep and the stars got up and I want to go to sleep and I followed the tracks into this tracks-tunnel and —'

'Say again, Jimmybuckle?'

'But the train went too fast —'

'No, about following the tracks into this —'

'I followed the tracks into this tracks-tunnel —'

'Train-tunnel. It's a train-tunnel,' said Supersonic.

'I followed the tracks into this train-tunnel and here

I am. Good night, Supersonic.'

Train-tunnel! It was a train-tunnel! And, thought Supersonic, when the train comes through this tunnel it's like nowhere else on earth — like nowhere except a train-tunnel, in fact. How could he not have known he was in a train-tunnel? Maybe he needed some sleep too. He did. A train-tunnel!

'Good night, Jimmybuckle,' he said.

'Will you roost beside me, Supersonic? This is my first night away from home.'

'No need to worry, young Jimmybuckle. It's all under control now. You roost here, on this stone by the wall — no, don't perch on the track, that's not a good idea — on the flat stone by the wall, and I'll roost beside you.'

'OK, Supersonic.' Jimmybuckle settled down on the stone.

'Sleep tight, young Jimmybuckle.'

But Jimmybuckle was already in dream-world and didn't hear.

It was night and no more trains came.

Follow the Tracks

~

They followed the tracks for three days. On the first day Supersonic's damaged wing was very sore, so he couldn't fly. On the second day it was very stiff, so he still couldn't fly. On the third day it was a little better, so he tried flying about fifty metres at a time, close to the ground. But most of the time they walked. They walked, beside the tracks, because Supersonic had come to the conclusion that the sky around those parts was the domain of the falcon.

Jimmybuckle never left Supersonic's side. Now that he had an older pigeon around to do his thinking for him, he was quite happy. He didn't seem to care how long the journey home took, as long as he could make it with Supersonic. Supersonic, for his part, was glad to be with a pigeon whom he could display his knowledge to, show off in front of, and hide his own fears from. Many trains passed them in both directions during those days, and Supersonic explained to Jimmybuckle that it was not always the same train — that there was more than one train in the world.

Sometimes, close to the tracks, there were fields and gardens where spring cabbage shoots grew, and Supersonic and Jimmybuckle raided these alongside the country pigeons and the country crows and jack-daws. These birds always kept a lookout for what they called 'humans with bangsticks', which sounded very much like the things Gerry called 'Hey-look-out-he's-got-a-gun' when he watched the thing called 'theTV'. The country birds were tense as trip-wires, ready to fly at the slightest noise, yet calm. They saw everything and missed nothing. This is the way you have to be if, at any second, your life can be ended by a shotgun, a falcon or a fox.

Supersonic hated the cabbage, disliked the seeds they found in the ploughed fields and wasn't too keen on the water of the gurgling streams where they drank. It was cold and clear and had no taste — it tasted like water. He would have swapped it all for one greasy chip and one slurp of a sweet fizzy drink. After three days of this diet, he did feel a lot calmer and more clear-headed than he ever had before; but calmness and clear-headedness weren't everything, he thought.

Nights in the countryside were full of sounds that Supersonic had never heard before: the lowing of cattle, the chirping of bats, hares screaming like human babies when they were caught by foxes. These noises would be explained by the country birds in the fields, the next day; but, in the night, even knowing what they were held little comfort. Roosting in a leafy bush or in the rafters of an old barn, Supersonic would put his good wing around Jimmybuckle and they would huddle together in the shadows.

During the hours before dawn, a silence would descend — an unusual silence, so quiet you could hear it. Then, instead of being a stranger in a strange place, Supersonic would feel that he was part of the night itself. His fears would vanish, his breathing would adjust to the rhythm of the countryside, and he would sleep.

At dawn he and Jimmybuckle would awaken, or be awakened by the chorus of the country birds, and another day would begin. Normally Supersonic liked to sleep a little later, but even he had to admit that the dawn chorus was beautiful. First, a lone blackbird would pipe up in the darkness; another would answer; and then others would join in, like the dead awakening. Then it was light. It was weird and glorious. Supersonic just wished they could have had a mid-morning chorus, or a noon chorus, instead of a dawn one.

☆

By the third day, Supersonic's clear-headedness was beginning to work in his favour. At dusk they were on the edge of a town, following the tracks as usual. There was a train on the tracks. It was standing still; it had stopped at the station.

Supersonic was looking at it. He was thinking, very clearly, 'This train is going to Dublin, and it's going there a lot faster than we can walk.'

He tested his wing — stiff and sore. He tested the feet he had been walking on for three days — nothing. They were beyond stiffness and soreness; they might as well have belonged to another pigeon. The choice was made.

'Jimmybuckle,' he said, 'follow me.'

He flew and Jimmybuckle, as ever, followed. It was just a short hop to the top of the train. Supersonic was expert at balancing on the handlebars of Gerry's bicycle. He showed Jimmybuckle how to grasp a bar going across the train and crouch low for balance. They waited, like sprinters down on the blocks, and after a time the train began to leave the station; slowly at first, then faster and faster, it followed the tracks followed the tracks followedthetracksfollowedthetracks —

The cold wind rushed by them; it was fiercer than when they flew, because now they were battling against it to keep balanced, rather than using it for their own advantage. They were so thrilled at being carried along by the train that they forgot they could fly almost as fast by themselves. 'Wheee! Arrhhh!' they shouted, as the train dipped and climbed and snaked its speedy way northwards. 'Wheee! Arrhhh!' Supersonic shouted, happy in the knowledge that no falcon was stupid enough to dive-bomb the train.

It was an exhilarating journey through the cold evening; and they were sorry it was over, but unbelievably glad to be back, when at last the train pulled in to the hustle and the bustle and the cars and the smoke and the streets of Dublin.

☆

They left the train when it slowed at a station in the city. First they flew to Jimmybuckle's loft. Supersonic's heart pumped with excitement. He had been half-expecting great outpourings of joy on his return to the city — fireworks, music, choirs of angels. In fact, despite all the bustle of the streets below, there was a calmness about Dublin that he had never seen before. Maybe it was his own calmness, brought back from the country-side? Or could it be the cold, breezy air of the young Spring making everything clear? At first Supersonic was disappointed, but then he began to feel that the

city was not ignoring him but waiting for him — waiting for him to return to his own home.

The time came to say goodbye to Jimmybuckle.

'I knew I'd be last,' said the younger pigeon, 'and I am last and I knew I would be.'

'Better last than never,' said Supersonic. 'Goodbye, Jimmybuckle.' And he flew quickly away.

But within seconds he turned and flew back.

'Hey, Jimmybuckle.'

Jimmybuckle had already started his descent. He flipped upwards and looked at Supersonic.

'You're not last, Jimmybuckle. You're second-last. I'm last.' And Supersonic spun around on his pale blue wings, using his spread tail-feathers as a rudder.

He had flown only a short distance when he heard a squeaky, breathless voice behind him. It was Jimmybuckle calling. Both pigeons circled in the warm, smoky air rising from a factory chimney.

'We're both last, Supersonic. We're last, but we're not least.'

'Hey, you're on to something there, Jimmybuckle.'

'Goodbye, Supersonic.'

'Last but not least. Last but — Jimmybuckle, you're all right. Yeah, you're all right, man.'

And they parted for the third time and flew to their separate homes.

Home for a While

~

It was twilight, and Spring blew a cold dry wind east-wards across Supersonic's path. He sped over familiar suburbs until he came to Ratheane. He flew over the village with its shops: the post office, the chipper, the kebab take-away, the Indian restaurant whose rubbish-bins were a treasure chest and always worth checking out. But not this evening.

Supersonic flew down the familiar road with its line of young sycamore trees. He looked to see if anything had changed. The trees had budded a little more; there were more of those yellow flowers that Gillian called 'mindmydaffodils'; but otherwise everything was the same. The street was empty of humans, but some could be seen by the yellow light inside their windows.

He came to Gerry's home and swooped low. There it stood, with the wind blowing darkness over it. A window was bright and yellow. Supersonic flew to it, stood on the sill and peered in, anxiously turning his head from side to side. Gerry's parents were watching the bright magical thing called 'theTV'. Supersonic couldn't see Gerry or June.

In a flapping whoosh, he flew around to the back of the house and swooped upwards, towards a window with a low golden glow. He stood on the sill and peered inside.

June lay on the bed in a pool of light, and Gerry sat on the floor with his head resting on the bed. Gerry's eyes were closed, and on his lap, moving up and down with each breath, was the music-making thing he called 'mytickettofameandfortune'.

Supersonic pecked on the window. There was no reaction. He pecked harder.

June sat up. She rubbed her eyes and looked at the door and then at the ceiling. Again Supersonic pecked on the window.

June turned a frightened face towards him, then jumped up on the bed and flew across the floor with one leap.

'Supersonic, you're back!' she cried, as she yanked the window open.

'Howya, June, greetings from the countryside,' said Supersonic as he flew into the warmth.

'*Supersonic!*'

'*Gerry!*'

'Supersonic! Mwa! mwa! mwa!'

'Don't *doo* that! That's my ear.'

'Supersonic, I knew you weren't dead.'

'Well, that's more than I knew for a lot of the time.'

'Sian Whelan! What does she know? I knew you were alive — knew it, knew it, knew it! He's alive. It's *Supersonic!*' Gerry shouted at June, as if she couldn't see for herself.

On the train journey and the flight over the city, when he'd known for sure that he would get home, Supersonic had allowed himself to imagine this moment. Now that it was here in reality, something was missing. What could make this better?

He flew to the table beside the bed. 'Crisps and Coke,' he said.

'See,' said Gerry, 'he's delighted to be home. What could have happened to him? How come he took so long?'

'Crisps and Coke,' said Supersonic, louder this time.

'He's supposed to be the fastest racing pigeon in the country.'

'How can he be fast? He only eats rubbish,' said June.

'He eats peanuts.'

'He should be eating vegetables,' June said.

'What kind of vegetables?'

'Cabbage, carrots, I don't know.'

'Would ya gimme a break! I hate cabbage. I've been eating cabbage all week. Get us some crisps,' said Supersonic.

'You think they'd help?' asked Gerry.

'I'm sure they would,' said June. 'You think Olympic athletes win gold medals on crisps and Coke?'

'I suppose you're right. Supersonic, it's cabbage and carrots for you from now on, and mineral water.'

'Make it tap water,' said June.

'Tap water.'

'*What*?' screamed Supersonic. 'I hate water. Water is for fish. Gimme some crisps and curry chips and Coke. If I wanted to eat cabbage, I'd have stayed in the countryside!'

'See, he's excited about it already,' said Gerry. 'Look at his feathers.'

'I think you should give him some Coke and crisps first. Just this once,' said June.

'That's more like it. That's a bit better.' Supersonic's feathers had become ruffled in his indignation. He shook them down and shifted from foot to foot. This only brought his indignation welling up again. 'My feet are killing me. I've been walking for three days. I've been attacked by a peregrine falcon. I come home and I get *cabbage*!'

'You were what?' June said.

'Attacked by a peregrine falcon. Well, what did you think happened? I went on me holidays?' Supersonic said.

'You're very cheeky for a bird that was supposed to win the race. Know how much money you won?' June asked.

'No.'

'None.'

'Gimme some crisps and Coke.'

'Crisps and Coke, crisps and Coke .... You know, I think you really are a parrot.'

'Nice to see you too, June.'

Gerry had been watching this conversation in wide-eyed, open-mouthed astonishment, turning his head from side to side like a spectator at a tennis match.

'You can understand what he's saying,' he said.

'Don't be silly,' June replied.

'You can. You were talking to him.'

'I was talking to myself.'

'June, you can understand birds! That's brilliant!'

'Is it?'

'You can talk to Supersonic! I can't do that. Can you teach me? I want to talk to him too.'

'Why does everyone want to talk to me and no one wants to give me *crisps and Coke*?'

'What's he saying? What were you saying to him just now?'

'I was .... He was telling me what happened.'

'What did happen?' Gerry asked.

'How did you escape, Supersonic?'

'Escape? Escape from what?' Gerry shouted.

Supersonic answered:

'Gave her the slip.

Falcon's thick.

Can't handle my tricks.

I am Super*sonic*!'

'You boaster,' said June. 'If you're so great, how come you didn't win a prize?'

'I was attacked by a falcon. If you have a complaint, take it up with her.'

'What's he saying? June, you're probably the only person in the world who can talk to birds — the only person in Ireland, anyway. What's he saying?'

June was staring at Supersonic, who was standing

on the table, looking at his reflection in the face of Gerry's alarm clock. She sat on the bed and looked up at her brother.

'He was attacked by a peregrine falcon. That's why he didn't win a prize.'

'Supersonic, you poor thing!' Gerry knelt down and kissed him on the head. 'Mwa! mwa!'

'Don't do that. That's my *ear*!'

'You could have been killed!'

'Gerry!' said June.

'What?'

'Remember what Uncle Jack said about falcons being worth loadsamoney?'

'Yeah, what about it?'

'Gerry?'

'What?'

Abruptly Gerry looked at June. She was working her tongue around inside her cheek, the way she always did when she was thinking about something.

'June? June!'

'Yes.'

'No way, June. It's illegal. You could go to jail for stealing a falcon.'

A smile spread, very slowly, from her lips to her eyes. 'Just think of all that money. And just think — if it hadn't been for that falcon, Supersonic would have won the race.'

'No way, June. No way. That's crazy. Besides, we don't know where the falcon is.'

'Yes we do.'

'No we don't.'

'Supersonic knows. Don't you know where the falcon is, Supersonic?'

'I have the map emblazoned on me heart,' said

Supersonic, who was mesmerised by the handsome reflection in the alarm clock. One thing puzzled him: when he raised his right wing, the pigeon in the clock raised his left wing. Supersonic didn't know the difference between left and right; but he did notice that, when he raised his sore wing, the pigeon in the clock raised a wing that, in Supersonic's body, was not sore. So the pigeon in the clock was not him. It was very puzzling. But it was fun.

'And you'll take us there.'

'Hah! That's good, that's very good. Nope. From now on, I'm a home-bird.'

'You'll take us.'

'Nope. I'll give that one a miss, if you don't mind. I'm not going anywhere near that falcon again — not now, not ever. Crisps and Coke.'

'What's he saying?' asked Gerry.

'He's, ah ....' June moved her tongue around in her cheek. Her eyes were still smiling. 'He's saying he thinks the cabbage is a great idea.'

'What?' said Supersonic.

'Yeah?' said Gerry.

'And that he'd like it boiled and left to cool for three days.'

'*June!*'

'And he doesn't want to drink Coke, or mineral water, or even tap water. He wants to drink the water the cabbage is boiled in — after it's been left to cool for three days, of course.'

'No problem, Supersonic,' said Gerry.

'June, don't *doo* this!'

'What's that?' said June. 'You'd like some cabbage now? I'm afraid we don't have any. You'll have to wait until tomorrow.'

'OK! I'll take you!'

'Of course you will,' June said. 'It's so much easier when we co-operate.'

'By the way,' said Supersonic, 'my wing is fine. Thanks for asking.'

It was then they noticed that he was standing sorrowfully with his right wing hanging down by his side.

Guardian of the Eyrie

~

'Kek kek kek.'

She was monarch of her territory, and she surveyed it with powerful forward-facing eyes. She stood in her eyrie, a scooped-out hollow in a rocky ledge on the wall of an inlet. Seen from above, she was blue with a steely sheen; from below, her powerful breast and the undersides of her wings were white with black bars. Her feet, the skin around her eyes, and the back of her beak were bright yellow. The tip of her beak was blue, and the upper part curved downwards in a razor-sharp hook. Her talons, too, were steel-blue meat-hooks.

'Kek kek kek,' she said again: a harsh, rattling cry. Though graceful in the air, she was awkward on the ground. She moved from side to side on her yellow legs, sometimes opening her wings for balance. She had a full crop from a kill the night before, but she was restless. Spring was moving through the countryside, whispering to her that it was time to lay eggs and raise chicks with her mate.

Far below, close to the water, she saw two he-humans and a she-human come out of the mouth of a big white beetle. The wind had not yet caught their smell; it carried only the scents of heather, flowers and the sea. The wind was to the falcon as water is to a fish — her natural element.

The thin he-human carried a pigeon. The falcon recognised the pigeon that had gone into the hole. The humans were looking towards her but also looking through her, in the manner of humans who could not see her at all. The falcon was used to this. She could make out every detail of their pink faces.

The pigeon was safe this morning, because he was with the humans. If he parted from them, though, she might dive on him, just for fun — or for real.

But it wasn't the pigeon who parted from the others. The she-human began to climb. She carried something. Every step of her climb, every rock and bush she grabbed hold of, every grimace and expression on her face, was watched by someone with powerful binoculars — the falcon's eyes. Sometimes the she-human would stop and look towards the falcon — and look through her.

'Kek kek kek.' The falcon was alarmed.

The she-human looked through the falcon again and changed direction slightly.

On and on she climbed.

'Kek kek kek.'

Again the she-human adjusted her direction. Why did she not move away from the falcon's voice, as every other creature in this territory did? She moved towards it. When she was in seeing range, she would know her mistake.

She was nimble and quick as a goat. Sometimes she would stop, look upwards and then bound forward by the easiest route over the rocks. When the climb was steep and dangerous, she slowed to a steady crawl.

On and on she climbed.

'Kek kek kek.'

The she-human stopped and looked. This time she did not look through the falcon. The strong eyes and the weak eyes met. Each saw the other.

On and on she climbed.

The weak eyes looked at the strong eyes, never wavering, never turning. Why did the weak eyes stare at the strong eyes so?

Could this be?

No. This was a human.

Beautiful eyes.

Go away.

'Kek kek kek.'

On and on she climbed.

She was by the eyrie.

'Kek kek kek.'

The she-human spoke. 'Don't be afraid.'

'Kek kek kek. Go away.'

'Don't be afraid. I'll go away soon.'

'Kek kek kek. Go away. *Go away*!'

But the friendly, fearless eyes never wavered.

'I'll go away soon. You can trust me. Don't be afraid.'

'I am not afraid of you, she-human.'

'Then why do you want me to go away?'

No. It was not possible. Did the she-human know her language? Surely no human knew the language of the birds?

'What is your name?' the she-human asked.

Test her.

'Longwing,' said the falcon.

'Longwing,' said the she-human.

Impossible. She understood.

'You understand me?' said Longwing.

'I understand all birds.'

'What are you called?'

'I am called June,' said the she-human.

'June,' said Longwing softly. 'June.'

'Wow,' said June. 'Look at the view from up here. It's beautiful.'

'This is my territory. I see for miles. Down there, by the black rock above the water — a mouse.'

The understanding she-human eyes looked down. 'I can't even see the rock,' she said.

'I know,' said Longwing.

'This is your territory?'

'My husband Bluebeak is hunting to the south. I am the guardian of the eyrie.'

'Guardian of the eyrie.' The she-human June moved higher. There was another ledge, above the eyrie, which protected it from the rain. 'Guardian of the eyrie,' she said again. 'It's so beautiful.'

Then the world went black.

Nodser

~

'No problem, Jack, whatsoever.'

Uncle Jack's 'contact', the man who would get money for the falcon, was called Nodser. He was small and wiry as a lightweight boxer. Like a boxer in the ring, he continually shifted his feet, jerked his shoulders to stop his jacket sliding off and twisted his head as if he had an irritating rash on the back of his neck. He hadn't shaved for days, so he had an even growth of spiky red hair on his skull and face. He spoke through his nose, in tandem with his boxerlike jerking, so that 'No problem, Jack, whatsoever' came out something like, 'Nho problem, *Jeck*, *whatsoever*.'

There was a blue tattoo on his forehead which many people stared at curiously. It seemed to be words, but they were impossible to make out from a distance. To read them you had to get closer, much closer — and this was what Nodser wanted. As the unsuspecting

eye moved within six inches of the blue tattoo, it would resolve itself into a stark question:

'What you looking at?'

Then Nodser would bop his bony forehead, tattoo and all, against the staring eye. He called this 'giving the nod', which is why he was called Nodser.

'Ya mean, *Jeck*, she climbed up the moun*tin*, put the boird in the *bag* and brought it *back* to the *van*?' said Nodser.

'I would have climbed up myself,' said Jack, 'but I had to mind the motor.'

'Plucky young wan, *all* the same. Plucky young wan,' Nodser repeated.

He jerked his head towards June and then back to Jack. 'I'll be round again to*morrow* with the *munee*. I'll collect the boird *then*. All *right*, *Jeck*?'

'Will she be all right?' asked June.

'Will who be all right, luv?' asked Nodser softly.

'Longwing. The falcon.'

'The boird is going to a good place. She shouldn't *worry*,' said Nodser, looking at Jack.

Nodser had called round to look at the falcon. He constantly referred to June as if she wasn't there. Another thing she disliked about him was his habit of calling her 'luv'.

They were in the kitchen. It was Tuesday of Easter week. June and Gerry were on holidays from school, and their parents were away in the hotel in the West. That morning June had taken Longwing from her eyrie.

'Well, I'll be *off*,' said Nodser.

'And you'll have the money tomorrow?' said Jack.

'Nho problem, *Jeck*, *what*so*ever*.'

There was an awkward silence.

'I'll — ah — be off too,' said Jack. He looked at June.

She was moving her tongue around inside her cheek. 'Are you eating well, June? Getting the proper vitamins and all?' he asked.

She didn't answer.

Jack looked at his watch. 'It's eight o'clock now — if you want me to stay and help you with the dinner ...?'

'You mean help us eat it?'

'No, no,' said Uncle Jack. 'It's just — if you're having your dinner soon — Nodser and myself are ....' His voice trailed off. Nodser jerked his head towards June, his upper lip twitching like a dreaming dog.

June fixed both of them with an even stare. 'We've already eaten,' she said. 'If either of you would like beans on toast, you're welcome to help yourselves.'

Jack and Nodser regarded each other for a moment; then both looked at June.

'No, no,' they said together.

'Thanks all the same,' said Jack.

'*Yeh*. Thanks very *much*,' said Nodser, 'but I'd better be *off*.'

'I'd better be off as well,' said Jack.

'You can see yourselves out, if you don't mind,' said June, using a cutting remark she had read in a book.

'Don't mind, not at all,' said Uncle Jack.

'Nho problem *what*so*ever*.'

Jack and Nodser left by the back door.

As soon as they had gone, June went to her room. Longwing was there, and she was desperately worried about the falcon's behaviour.

Supersonic was standing on the bedside table in Gerry's room, shivering with fear. He had seemed to shrink in size when Gerry came in, as if fearing that Longwing might swoop through the opened door. He could never be happy sharing the house with a peregrine falcon, his deadliest natural enemy.

Gerry sat on the bed, strumming his guitar. Supersonic crooned along to the music, giving voice to his thoughts:

'There's a killer in the house.

My brain is squirming like a louse.

You must send her on the wing

For my misery to end.

Killer in the house.

Killer in the house!'

Gerry strummed his guitar absent-mindedly. Sometimes he would forget his thoughts in favour of his strumming and practice a new chord sequence. But mostly the guitar was a prop that he used to help him think, the way June stared out of windows and moved her tongue around in her cheek when she had something on her mind.

Gerry would have preferred it if falcons didn't attack Supersonic, but he felt that in taking Longwing from her eyrie they had done something appallingly wrong. Now that Nodser was on the scene, things seemed to have spun out of control, and Gerry wasn't sure how to put them right. He had wanted to stop June — he still did — but she was so headstrong ....

He looked at Supersonic crooning along to the music. Supersonic, he knew, was terrified of the peregrine. If June had been there, she would have known exactly what Supersonic was saying. Gerry pondered the injustice of it: he, who loved birds, couldn't understand them, and June, who could understand them, didn't seem to care for them at all.

'Crroo-coo-hoo-hoose,' Supersonic seemed to say.

Gerry listened intently. He began to keep time with Supersonic, letting him lead. He forgot himself and became lost in the guitar and Supersonic.

'Hoose — hoose — house,' Supersonic sang. 'Hares hah hill her hin hah house. Hares a killher hin the house.'

What? *What*?

He had heard Supersonic sing, 'There's a killer in the house.'

Gerry stopped his guitar-strumming to listen; but immediately he was catapulted back to the human world, and from there Supersonic seemed only to make his gurgling crooning sounds. He tried and tried and tried to understand Supersonic again; but instead of listening to Supersonic, he was listening to himself telling himself to listen. It was only after a long time — when, tired and frustrated, he forgot himself again — that he made any progress.

A Small Space

~

When the darkness had come in the eyrie, Longwing
had stayed silent. The soothing voice of the she-human
June remained close by. Longwing felt herself being
handled and carried and bumped and buffeted. She
was inside something loose and strong. This lasted for
a long time. She did not, could not, fly. She stayed
silent; alert, awake — waiting.

The light returned in an instant, flash-bright. She
found herself squeezed in a place without space, in
between walls that had no in-between. The walls were
the colour of the sunrise and as slippery as the sea.
When she moved her head to the left, they lurched
stomach-churningly to the right. She swirled right to
still the walls, but instead they rushed leftwards,
dancing round her, crowding and trapping her. Shapes
jumped and flashed at her out of the sunrise swirl. The
she-human June lunged at her and disappeared. She

dared not risk flight here.

'Kek kek kek.'

'Longwing!' It was the she-human's voice. June flew into vision, this time from the opposite direction, and disappeared again. Then she was back. Steady.

Longwing's eyes settled on the figure of June.

There was the she-human, in the wall.

No.

There was the she-human, and the wall was apart from her and behind her. The surfaces she was between began to broaden out into space. As a human looking through binoculars in a small room must adjust the focus, so Longwing adjusted the focus of her own eyes. There was June, close by, and the wall, not so close. But everything was close. She was trapped in a space tinier than any she had ever seen.

She flew.

But there was no place to fly to. She could only fly round and round the small space. She saw another falcon in the wall — not apart from the wall this time; definitely in the wall. Was it Bluebeak, her husband? Her heart soared. She flew to him and he flew to her. He looked different — bigger than normal. He was trapped in a hole in the wall. Something hard and smooth stopped her from entering it.

'Bluebeak! Bluebeak!' she cried.

'No, stop! Stop, Longwing!' June shouted.

'Bluebeak? *What have you done to him*?'

'That's not Bluebeak! That's *you* — look.'

And June took the hole out of the wall and carried it in her hands.

'Look,' she said, 'it's your reflection. In the mirror. It's a mirror.'

'Mirror,' said Longwing. She saw her reflection as she had seen her reflection in water, except that this was perfectly clear. Now June was in the mirror — now Longwing — now both. Longwing and June looked at themselves in the mirror.

'Longwing — June,' said June to the mirror.

'Longwing — June,' said Longwing to the mirror.

'Yes,' said June, 'it's our reflection.'

'I want Bluebeak,' said Longwing.

'Do you miss him?' asked June.

'Yes.'

'I can get him for you.'

'*No!*'

Longwing looked without interest at her reflection.

'I didn't think of that,' said June. 'I didn't think you'd miss him. I'm sorry, Longwing .... Look!' June hung the mirror back on the wall and reached underneath the table where Longwing stood. She brought out a globe. 'Look, Longwing. This is the Earth. Well, it's like the Earth, same as your reflection is like you. This is a reflection of the Earth. Here's Ireland, where we are.' She pointed to a green dot on the globe. 'How would you like to go' — June twirled the globe — 'all the way across to here — to Arabia, where it's always warm — and live in a big palace with a prince?'

'I want to go to my territory.'

'But you can have another territory. In Arabia. It's beautiful there. You'll love it when you get there. You really will. Longwing, you'll love it. Trust me.'

'You said that before,' Longwing replied, without looking at her.

☆

Those were the last words she had spoken.

She was also refusing food and drink.

That morning, after bringing her to the house, June had tried to tempt her with chicken nuggets — which

she herself loved. Longwing had ignored them with the disdain of a cat being offered burnt toast. Coke, Supersonic's favourite tipple, was similarly scorned. Thinking that Longwing might have more natural tastes, June had offered her water and some uncooked chicken breast that Gillian had left in the fridge for June and Gerry to cook while she was away.

Longwing hadn't looked at it.

Throughout the day, June had coaxed and pleaded with Longwing to eat, and especially to drink. But the magnificent bird had no interest in food or drink or anything — not even in life, it seemed.

And June didn't know what to do.

Moonflight

~

Often people with special talents don't appreciate them at first.

This had been the case with June when she had first become aware she could understand birds. Then, in the past few weeks — first with Supersonic, now with Longwing — she had begun to see just how unusual her ability was. No sooner had she realised this than her talent disappeared: neither Supersonic nor Longwing would talk to her any more. June thought Supersonic was protesting because she had brought a falcon into the house, but Longwing's silence was more worrying.

Some people understand cars, or horses, or computers, so well that it's as if they can talk with them. June had come to understand birds so well that she really could talk to them. When she spoke with Supersonic and Longwing, it was as if she stopped being an eleven-year-old girl and became a bird. She was tuned in to a secret — ancient, mysterious, alien — which no one else she knew was privy to. It was as if she was the only person in the room who could see a ghost; and she had been frightened.

Gradually, though, her fear had been replaced by excitement. Being able to talk with a creature as wild and proud as Longwing had given her a thrill like nothing else in the world. Even climbing up to the eyrie, doing something she knew she shouldn't do, had made her feel like a bandit queen of old.

But now it was all going wrong.

When Nodser and Uncle Jack left, June rushed up to her room. Longwing stood on the table, in the same position where June had left her earlier. She swayed from side to side, her wings hanging slack like a blue sheet draped loosely over her shoulders. Her eyes, black and blank as eye-holes cut in a mask, stared ahead. Longwing stood behind a steel wall of silence, and with every passing second she withdrew further from June. She was drifting into another world, and June had a dread of what this other world might be.

'Longwing, please eat. If you don't eat or drink, you'll die.' The masklike eyes gave no indication that they could see June; but neither did they give any sign that they didn't register every detail of June, of the room, and of the darkening sky beyond the window. 'I don't want you to die. I want you to talk to me. Won't you talk to me?'

Silence.

'Please, Longwing.'

Silence.

'I'll take you back to your territory tomorrow. Now won't you talk to me?'

Silence.

'Longwing, I'll take you back. Trust me.'

As soon as June had said this, she blushed bright red. Did Longwing notice? There was no sign that she did — or that she didn't. But Longwing couldn't trust her; June had broken her trust that morning in the eyrie.

And June wasn't sure she could be trusted, either. She wasn't at all sure that she would be able to take Longwing back. Had it been just Uncle Jack she was dealing with, it wouldn't have been a problem. But Nodser was different. There was something vicious about him. He wanted to make money by selling Longwing, and he wouldn't take kindly to being denied.

Maybe she should let Longwing go now? No, she couldn't let her go at night. In the morning, then? But would she be able to get back to her territory? Did falcons have a homing instinct, like pigeons? June didn't know. Was there anyone she could ask? Uncle Jack? No, he wouldn't have a clue ....

The money wasn't important any more. She would rather have Longwing talk to her. Or even Supersonic.

The day after Supersonic returned, June had told Sian Whelan in school, 'He's not dead. He came back last night.'

Sian had looked at her with mocking cat's-eyes. 'And you're happy about that?' It was impossible to tell if she was being sarcastic or was genuinely surprised at June being pleased. 'My dad calls them flying rats. He says they carry disease and shouldn't be let in the house. You'll probably end up infecting us all with the plague or something.'

Jennifer Adams had been there at the time. She said she'd heard that too: 'I've heard of pigeons carrying disease.' Sian had looked at her, surprised — Jennifer wasn't usually on her side — but June had thought that even her best friend was making fun of her.

'Yes, I've heard that pigeons can carry disease. So can cats and dogs. It's present in their droppings.' Jennifer had said the word 'droppings' very politely, like an aristocratic lady announcing tea. 'Pigeon droppings are called guano. I'll spell it: g-u-a-n-o. So if anyone has had pigeon guano dropped on her head recently, she could be in trouble. She might want to get her head examined.'

Both Sian and June had been amazed. They hadn't known Jennifer to be this cutting for ages. It was like she was becoming her old self again. But June remembered that Sian had also looked worried. She must have thought she really did need to get her head examined after Supersonic had dropped his guano on it.

June was sure that, for all Sian's coolness and money, she would never know what it was like to talk with a magnificent bird like Longwing in her own eyrie. She felt herself blush again at the memory of how she had lied to Longwing. She would make it up to her in the morning. She would.

A horrible thought came to her. What if Longwing died in the night?

'Longwing, don't die. Tomorrow you'll be in your eyrie. Longwing?'

Silence.

Longwing wouldn't talk to her. Supersonic wouldn't talk to her. Gerry was annoyed with her. Her parents were away. And if they had been there, they wouldn't have let her do what she'd done. She couldn't talk to Jennifer, because she would be horrified.

When June had carried Longwing in, in a bag, that morning, Jennifer had been in her garden next door holding a ladder for her father, who had been nervously cleaning their upstairs windows. June had shouted a hasty 'Hi,' and rushed inside. She felt sure that Jennifer suspected something was going on. How could she have got into this mess? And how could she get out of it?

'It's all right for you, Longwing,' she said. 'You look cool all the time. You don't need clothes. You have beautiful feathers. You can fly.'

Longwing's depthless dark eyes stared towards the window.

'That's what I do.' June began to undress and put on her pyjamas. 'I'm always looking out windows.'

She opened the window a fraction, to let the air in, and climbed in between the clean cotton sheets. Her bed stood between the window and the table. She hadn't put the light on, but the moon had positioned itself so close outside her window that it seemed she could have hit it with a stone. To see the face in the moon, June always had to remember a cartoon drawing she had seen of it. She pictured this drawing now, and there was the face in the real moon, looking to the right. Her room, with its primrose-yellow walls, was transformed into a milky-blue vault. On the table, Longwing stood looking across the bed towards the moon. A light wisp of cloud slipped over its face, giving it a rainbow halo. Ring Out Your Great Bells In Victory: Red, Orange, Yellow, Green, Blue, Indigo, Violet — they were all there, but it was hard to see the different colours if you didn't know them to start with.

'Long ago there was a city called Rome,' June said to Longwing. 'Well, there still is; but long ago, on moonlit nights, the Romans worshipped the goddess Juno. The month of June is named after Juno, and I'm named after the month of June, so I'm really named after a goddess of ancient Rome. A fortune-teller called Shahin told me that once.'

On the table beside her, Longwing stood still and

silent as a statue. She seemed to glow in the moonlight, as if she were made of sapphire like Shahin's talisman. June turned her head away towards the window, but she still felt the eyes of the falcon on her — eyes that were no longer the dead eyes of a mask, for now in each one glittered a little silver moon.

'In Rome there was a temple built to honour Juno, and in this temple there lived a flock of geese to keep Juno company — like you're keeping me company now, Longwing. The Gauls tried to invade the city once, by creeping up on it in the night. But Juno's geese heard them, and they started to cackle. They cackled so loudly that the Roman soldiers woke up and drove off the invaders.'

June lay on the bed, watched by moons that have watched the earth for millions of years — the moon outside her window, and the moons that glitter in a falcon's eyes.

She knew an ancient secret. Aided by imagination or memory, people can travel to distant lands and other times without ever leaving their rooms. They think that it is only they who can do this — that it is only humans who can escape from reality.

They are wrong. It is only they who need to do this. For birds, the world is a place of strangeness and mystery that forever excites their curiosity. They are never dull if they are free to follow their own natures. For birds, the moon can be a friend who calls to you in the night. Its face can be the handsome face of the young warrior Spring, whispering to you to fly to him. June was surrounded by reflections of this face — outside her window, in the mirror on the wall, and in Longwing's eyes.

She felt those eyes on her, and the falcon's silent breathing matching her own. Two little silver coins sparkled in June's eyes too. She perched on the bed, gazing at the face as it called softly, 'Fly to me.'

She arched her wings in one slow silent beat, luxuriating in their power. Behind her, Longwing unfolded her wings in a whiplash beat in preparation for flight.

The beautiful spring moon called again, 'Fly to me.'

If she flew, could she ever return again? She was afraid. June had become a falcon.

'Fly with me,' said Longwing. 'I will bring you back.' And Longwing flew to the window, which opened wide before her.

June watched her go, silent as an owl. She spread her own wings. She flew.

The night was still, and Ratheane was bathed in a patchwork of brightness and inky shadow. There was nothing underneath her keeping her up. She flapped her wings to stay afloat, like a poor swimmer splashing beyond her depth.

Longwing flew beside her and showed her how to move with glides and quick wingbeats. June began to trust her wings. She was free of roads and routes and obstacles. Her element was the air which carried her over everything, directly to where she wanted to go. She swam through the night air.

They moved over the enormous Christmas tree of bright and black that was the city. They flew on, out to the countryside, which was stripped of its green tonight and bathed in the same milky blue that had been in June's room. Now that the shakiness was gone, June began to experience the full thrill of flight. The Spring was happy to have Longwing and June fly to him.

'Look,' he said to them, 'look at what I do while the humans sleep.' June looked down, a mile or miles down. The cows, the sheep and their young lambs, the grass, the leaves, the foxes — the earth murmured with

their breath. 'Everything is growing,' said Spring. 'I breathe — life.' And he blew a sweet breeze over the countryside.

They flew on across the neverending, star-littered dome. June's wings carried her effortlessly over sea and mountains, valleys and fields. When they came at last to Longwing's territory, June realised that she had known all along that this was where they were flying to; but, in a strange way, she hadn't been aware of it until they got there. Time looked different when you were a falcon. You seemed to look down on it from above, rather than forward or back to it.

They criss-crossed the territory from east to west to east, moving south as they flew. Longwing showed June the abandoned old eyrie where she had been hatched and raised. She showed her the stream where she bathed her feathers and the inlet where she had killed her first duck.

They flew inland, still going south, until they came to an old church on a hill, on whose belltower Longwing had met Bluebeak. They landed on the tower and Longwing told June the story.

She had been resting there one day when Bluebeak had flown by. They had both been young falcons then, and he had tried to impress Longwing with his aerial acrobatics, doing somersaults and slick spirals before landing on the tower beside her. She had still been feigning indifference to his charms when the bells had rung out and they had flown off in fright.

That had been countless moons ago. They had raised three broods since then. What had June been doing on that day, years before, as Longwing and Bluebeak met? Probably she had been at school ....

Lastly they flew back north, and from on high they saw Bluebeak alone in the eyrie. He stood, etched sorrowfully against the rocks, with his wings slack by his sides. June the falcon knew Longwing would have to go to him.

'Goodbye, Longwing,' said June.

'I must take you back, June.'

'Aren't you going to Bluebeak?'

'I must take you back. You cannot return without me.'

And in the same way as June had known where they were headed without being fully aware of it, she knew that she must return to her home — and very quickly.

When we sleep, our spirits leave our bodies — usually to live in dreams, but in June's case that night, to fly over the countryside as a falcon. While we sleep, we like to deposit our bodies in secure places — in beds in quiet rooms — where they will be safe until we return to them in the morning. Usually our spirits stay close by in space and travel in time, as when we dream of the past. But that night June's spirit had strayed far from her body in space. She knew her human body was back in her bedroom, and she began to feel a terrible lonesomeness for it.

At this time of the year the sun shining through her window woke her at dawn. June knew — she didn't know how she knew, but she did — that if her spirit had not returned to her sleeping body by the time the sun was due to awaken her, she could never return. She would remain a falcon, which was bearable; but what she could not bear was the thought of Gerry finding her body dead in her bed.

For the first time June saw the awful risk she had taken in choosing to fly out the window as a falcon. With rising panic, she realised that she was totally dependent on Longwing to return her to herself.

Longwing had read June's panic before she herself felt it.

'Follow me,' she said. It never seemed to occur to her not to return June home.

'What about Bluebeak?' June asked.

They looked down at the eyrie. Bluebeak had his head raised, watching them. Watching them as they flew away.

'We must hurry,' was all that Longwing said.

A breeze was helping them along, but the air was dusty and unclear. Longwing flew ahead, using glides and quick silent wingbeats. Twice June lost sight of her in the dusty air and screamed out in fear, only to find that Longwing was right by her side.

They flew into the morning. 'Look,' said Spring, flinging away his blue cloak, 'I'm going to wear a shirt the colour of your bedroom walls.'

'No!' June screamed.

'Faster,' Longwing called. She increased her speed and June, tired and choking with the dust, tried to follow.

They saw the city silhouetted on the horizon, and June knew the yellow dawn would reach it first. The race was lost.

'Stoop,' Longwing screamed to her. '*Now!*'

Ever since Uncle Jack had told her about the spectacular falcon stoop, June had wanted to see it. Now she had to do it herself, to save her own life. But she couldn't just hurl herself towards the earth. If she did, she would die as a falcon too.

'Wait!' she called out to Longwing.

But Longwing was already half a mile below.

Then something happened to June. When a falcon stoops, it is hunting prey; and this instinct to hunt and kill chilled June's blood, vanquishing her nerves and giving her the courage to fold her wings and let gravity claim her. Her body rocked in the air as she sliced through it.

Longwing dived like a bomber jet, screaming towards earth.

'Pull out!' June yelled. 'Stop! You're going to crash!'

But the jet that Longwing had become didn't pull out of its dive. It crashed, in an orange explosion which pumped smoke as black as oil up into the sky.

June rushed to the explosion. She found herself on the ground, without wings, running on her own legs down her own road to the smoking ruins of her own house in Ratheane.

Where was Longwing?

Had she become the plane whose crash had destroyed every house on the road? But there was no sign of a plane either. There was only the débris of houses — and the people in the houses were acting as if nothing had happened.

There was Sian Whelan, playing a computer game on her smashed computer in her roofless bedroom. She was covered in dust and grime, but she didn't even notice. Her father came up to her and ruffled her hair. 'Dad, leave my hair *alone*!' she shrieked. But her hair looked like a stiff mop.

There was Jennifer Adams, calmly eating cornflakes amidst the rubble of her kitchen. And next door, June's own mother was hanging curtains in the gaping hole that had once been the living-room window. June wanted to tell her that the house had been destroyed, but the words wouldn't come.

There was Ben in the kitchen. He was telling Gerry about their trip to the castle hotel in the West, and explaining why they had come back early. The ceiling had fallen in — the whole upstairs had fallen in.

Supersonic was on Gerry's shoulder. Only he seemed to notice something amiss.

June couldn't bear it any longer. She looked at the

sun. She wanted to be a falcon and fly towards it. But she had no wings, only hands. She tried to flap her hands, but something soft and loose restrained them. She tried again. Her hands were tangled in cloth — a sheet? She flung it away.

The sun shone in her face. It was framed in a window. June sat up. She was in her bed, in her room. The walls glowed yellow. It was morning.

Morning? She turned sharply. Longwing was on the table, but not in the pitiful position of the night before. Now she stood serene as a queen.

'Longwing.'

'June.' She spoke!

'Longwing. Longwing, we flew. We went to your territory.'

'My territory?'

'Last night. You took me back.' Then June remembered the plane crash and the ruined houses. It had all been a dream .... No. It had been too real.

She looked the other way. The window was open wide.

The window was open wide!

She had flown in the night.

She hopped out of bed. It was 6.30 in the morning.

'June,' said Longwing.

'Yes?'

'I'm hungry.'

'Oh, Longwing.'

June rushed through her miraculously restored house to the kitchen. She got a raw chicken breast from the fridge and a bowl of water from the tap. Longwing ate and drank greedily.

'Longwing, you're so beautiful.'

Longwing had mantled her wing-feathers tentlike over her food. She glanced briefly at June. 'So beautiful,' she said. It was impossible to tell if she was referring to

June or to the food.

The memory of the night flight and the crash, and the people unaware that their houses were ruined, was vivid in June's mind. What was it trying to tell her? She was too jumpy to write it down in her notebook. She had to find out what it meant. The strange thing was that parts of it seemed familiar to her: the sapphire-blue falcon; walking through ruins where she had crash-landed ....

She went to the window and closed it. She had had an idea.

'Longwing, today you're going back to your territory. But first I have to go see someone.'

June put on jeans, runners and a T-shirt and ran downstairs to the kitchen again. She ate a quick bowl of cereal; then she wrote Gerry a note telling him where she was going, so he wouldn't be worried, and left it on the kitchen table.

Out of habit, she had put on the radio — her parents always liked to have the radio on in the morning. On the news, it said that all the cars in the city were covered in a fine red dust that morning. A balmy wind had blown up from Africa in the night, carrying with it dust from the Sahara Desert. The newsreader said that it happened every few years.

June couldn't believe that dust from the Sahara Desert could be blown all the way to Ireland. Then she remembered how the air had become dusty as they had flown. She put on her denim jacket and rushed outside.

All the cars were covered in a very fine red dust.

Shahin

~

The address was for a house on the seafront. There was a small round tower opposite it, and only a road, busy with morning traffic, separated it from the strand and its squabbling gulls. It was surprising how big gulls were when you saw them up close. Out on the sea June saw a ferry, very white in the morning sun, on its way to Wales. The open space here by the sea reminded her of Longwing's eyrie and of the vast space she and Longwing had flown across last night. Or dreamt of?

DING .... Silence .... DONG.

In a normal week, June would have been going to school now. She was happy to be free to go where she pleased on such a beautiful morning.

'Uh-huh.' She heard the key turning in the lock. The door opened.

'Hello.'

'Huh? Hum in.'

'I'm June Corcoran.'

'No.'

'I am.'

'Hi no. Hum in, Hune.'

June stepped into a warm, bright hallway. 'I came to see you about —'

'Hmm.'

'— a dream.'

The door closed behind her. 'Hoffee. Hum on.' The figure in the too-short blue dressing-gown — it didn't even reach his knees — trudged off down the hall and disappeared. June followed.

People know their own houses best, except in one important way: every house has a special smell, which outsiders catch straight away but which people living there are used to and don't notice any more. Shahin's house smelt of wood-smoke (maybe he burned log fires at night?) and of something exotic and tingly, like cinnamon. June passed a seven-foot-high plant with clumps of long, pointed leaves, which she recognised as a yucca plant. She had seen yucca plants before, in office windows and shopping centres, but they had never been this big.

She walked on into the kitchen. It was bright and very clean. The window over the sink revealed a jungle of shrubs and bushes, grass not cut since the Ice Age, nettles and, here and there, a stubborn and very determined flower. But the marvel of the garden was an enormous, drooping cherry tree, whose flowery branches formed a pink snowstorm frozen in mid-air.

June would have expected Shahin to have a more exotic dressing-gown (satin, maybe?); but no, it was cotton and looked like it had taken one spin too many round the washing machine. His kitchen did have a counter rather than a table, though, and he was making coffee in one of those cafetière plunger-things. He poured a mug for June and one for himself. The words 'We can't all be sex symbols' were printed on Shahin's lime-green mug. He saw that June had noticed this. 'Birthday gift,' he said, and shrugged.

June, who didn't know what to say, nodded politely.

Shahin took a satisfying gulp from his mug. 'Ahh!' he said. 'I am afraid I am a newborn puppy in the morning. My eyes will not open.' He took another gulp. 'That is better. June Corcoran, yes? I remember you, most certainly. Most certainly, yes. The girl who rescued my talisman.'

'Sorry for calling so early,' June said.

'Not at all, not at all.'

'I got your address from the sign in the arcade.'

'Ah, yes,' Shahin said. 'A pity about that place. I liked it. Still — progress .... We must make do. I work from here now.'

'It's beautiful,' June said.

'Thank you. Thank you. Yes.'

'I love the cherry blossom.'

'Oh, yes, the cherry blossom. Lovely.' Shahin took a sideways peep at the cherry blossom and gulped down more coffee.

Outside in the garden, the birds sang furiously. June heard one male blackbird sing to another that the garden of the cherry blossom was *his* territory, and that, if his rival entered it, he would risk having his gizzard

'... ripped asunder

And fed to the maggots of the bright blue yonder.

Come in, why don't you, and you will die;

Your blood will thicken and your bones will dry.'

In the next breath he called invitingly to any passing female blackbird who might like to have her nest in the beautiful garden of the cherry blossom:

'Come, my darling, and we will kiss,
And build a nest and raise our chicks.
A thing, O Beauty, you cannot miss:
A cherry blossom, a life of bliss!'
A blue-tit, a robin and a wren echoed similar tunes to
their own kinds, but none was as melodious as the
blackbird's song.

'Every morning, same thing.' Shahin looked out of
the window. '"Come in why don't you and you will die
your blood will blah blah blah." Or else, "Come in my
darling and we will smoochy smoochy smoochy."
Every morning, crack of dawn. I tell them: why not do
it later, their threatening and courting? But no. They
must do it at dawn. Why do I play my rotten music
late at night when they are trying to sleep, they say.
Help yourself to more coffee,' Shahin said, and he went
off muttering the word 'shower'. Whether he was
going to have one, or whether he was calling the birds
a 'shower' of something, wasn't clear. What was clear
was that, when Shahin listened to the birds, he heard
the same things June heard. He could understand their
language.

For some reason June had thought that Shahin, being
from India, would drink tea rather than this richly
aromatic coffee. She knew she shouldn't do it, but, to
satisfy her curiosity (she told herself it might give her
some interesting observations for her notebook), she
had a look in his cupboards. They were a jumble of
pots, mugs, jugs, plates, bags of pasta and rice and
noodles, herbs, spices, tins of tomatoes and, in one
cupboard, a box of tea bags marked 'Assam'. Beside
this lay a chunky set of keys, and next to these was an
airtight jar marked 'Tea'. June nodded. He did drink
tea. Probably he drank tea at night and coffee in the
morning.

But the airtight jar did not have tea in it. Lying at the bottom of the jar were photographs — the Polaroid snapshots that Shahin took of people when he told their fortunes. There were three of them.

June shook the jar so that she could make out all three faces. One face bore a close resemblance to a scowling turnip. She recognised the man as a politician whom she had seen on the TV but whose name she didn't know. The second face was also male — thin, with roundy glasses and a very self-important expression.

The third face belonged to Jennifer Adams.

There was no mistaking her. She was wearing the bold, reluctant expression she always wore when being photographed. She used to claim she was like certain Native American tribes who didn't like having their photographs taken, in case their spirits were robbed in the process. This had been before she became sensible; now she just thought photographs were a waste of time and money.

But what was her photograph doing in Shahin's jar?

June heard a noise in the hall. She closed the cupboard and was back on the other side of the counter when Shahin returned. She didn't have to use the excuse she'd thought of — that she'd been 'looking for biscuits'.

Shahin, his hair glistening from the shower and tied in a ponytail, now wore baggy green trousers and a white shirt. He looked quite tubby, but his face, which was golden-brown and dominated by a hooked nose, gave the impression that he should have been thin. He had put on a beautiful aftershave that had the same exotic scent June had noticed when she entered the house. She clutched her mug with both hands and tried to think why Shahin might have a photograph of Jennifer Adams in an airtight container next to his tea bags.

'This dream,' he said. 'Would you like to tell me about it?'

Before June had time to begin her story (and she wasn't sure where to begin), Shahin stuck his head out the window and shouted, 'Shut up, stupid blackbird!'

From amongst the cherry blossoms the blackbird called, 'Get lost, sleepyhead!'

'You get lost. It's my garden,' Shahin replied.

'No it's not, it's my territory,' called the blackbird, 'and any trespassers will have their gizzards ripped asunder and fed to —'

'Yes, yes, I know,' said Shahin, 'fed to the maggots of the bright blue yonder, same thing every morning.' He closed the window. 'The dream?'

'You can talk to birds.'

'Anyone can talk to birds. People talk to ducks and pigeons in the park all the time.'

'Yes, but —' June stopped herself. She wanted to say, 'But they don't understand when the ducks and pigeons talk back,' but to say this would reveal that she too understood birds. Instead she told Shahin about her dream.

June felt possessed by a strange power this morning — similar to what she felt when she talked to birds, but sharper. At the end of her dream (or moonflight?), what had given her the courage to begin her stoop was the hunter's instinct. That feeling of being on the hunt had stayed with her. It was as if she could concentrate her mind like a laser beam, ignoring all distractions — the kind of thing she could never do at school.

She began telling her dream, very clearly, and found that Shahin's attitude matched her own. He sat on a high stool behind the counter, his thin face and hooked nose pointing towards June. She had intended to tell him about the dream alone, but she found it hard to do that without mentioning Longwing. Shahin sat so silently, watching so intently, that soon June found herself telling him all about Longwing and how she had come to be in June's room the night before. His expression never changed, and he didn't say a word. He seemed able to read her mind, so that it was pointless trying to hide anything.

She finished by telling him about walking down her own road with the houses reduced to rubble. She said it had reminded her of something. From other visits to Shahin, June had learned to connect her dreams to things that happened to her while she was awake.

'What did it remind you of?'

'The last time I went to see you in the arcade, it was deserted and I was the only person there, and I felt like my spacecraft had crash-landed on another planet.'

'I see. Is that why you came to see me?'

'Yeah — I suppose so.'

'There is another reason?' June nodded her head. 'Tell it to me,' Shahin said gently.

'Last night, before I — before I went to sleep, Longwing reminded me of your statue, the talisman, the one that all the trouble was about that time.'

Shahin got up and quietly left the room. A few seconds later he came back, holding the bird-of-prey statue, which June now recognised as a falcon — a falcon made of a dark blue translucent stone. That time, weeks before, when Jennifer had tried to steal it, June had been so anxious to bring it back that she had hardly looked at it. Now she couldn't take her eyes off it.

Shahin handed it to her. While Longwing measured from about June's elbow to the tips of her fingers, this was barely the size of her fist; yet it was as heavy as a lump of metal. She examined it. It had a blue metal base. It was unbelievably beautiful.

She placed it on the counter. 'I thought you didn't like people touching it,' she said.

'You have touched it before, when you brought it back to me. Remember?' June said she did remember. 'You know the language of the birds, don't you, June? Earlier you knew that I was talking *with* the blackbird and not *to* him.'

'You know their language too,' June said. 'I thought I was the only one.'

Shahin laughed. 'No, not the only one. One of the few. One of the very few.'

He pointed to the statue. 'How do you like my shahin?' he asked.

'Your Shahin? You *are* Shahin.'

'In India, peregrine falcons are called shahin falcons. When I was a boy I had a falcon, so people called me Shahin.'

'You had a falcon? Are you a prince?'

'No, no.' He laughed. 'My family was very poor. I lived in a place called Rajasthan, which is in the north-west of India. There is much desert where I grew up. Food is scarce. I used my falcon to hunt for food — or, rather, my falcon would hunt for herself and share it with me.' Shahin was gazing upwards, as people do when they remember something from long ago. He stroked the statue gently with his hand. 'So I am named after a falcon and you are named after a goddess in ancient Rome,' he said, smiling.

It seemed to June that he was talking to her now as an equal — someone who could understand the language of the birds — and not as a little girl.

'Do you remember what I once told you about Juno's geese warning Rome it was under attack?' June said she did. Shahin seemed to remember everything. 'Well, once people put a poison called DDT on crops, to kill insects. It was thought to be harmless to humans, but birds like pigeons ate the crops, and falcons ate the pigeons. At each step on the food chain, the poison got stronger. Falcons are at the top of their food chain, and they started to die. Their eggs would not hatch. Sometimes they would be unable to pull out of their stoops and they would crash straight to the ground — like the plane Longwing became in your dream. It was the death of the falcons that warned people of the dangers of DDT. In many parts of the world it is now banned. As Juno's geese warned Rome, the falcons warned the world that it was under attack.'

'Is that what my dream meant? The end, when Longwing became a plane and crashed into the ground?'

'Possibly.'

'But I didn't know about all this — poison, and the falcons dying — until now.'

'In your dream, everything was destroyed. But no one noticed. No one cared. Except you. You have been given a clever dream.'

June thought about this. 'I shouldn't have taken Longwing from her eyrie,' she said. Shahin shrugged his shoulders. She got no feeling of disapproval from him. It was as if he had already forgiven her. 'What did the beginning of the dream mean? When I went flying with Longwing?'

'That was not the beginning of your dream. Your dream began when Longwing turned into a plane and crashed into the ground and you ran down the ruins of your own road. That was the beginning of your dream.'

'No,' June said. 'I flew with Longwing to her territory before that.'

'You flew with Longwing to her territory, but it was not a dream.'

'What do you mean?'

'It was not a dream.'

'Was it real?' June asked.

'We both know that, to talk to birds, one must enter their world — in some way become as a bird. Some people would say that what we do is not real, but that is only because they cannot do it themselves.' A patient smile spread across Shahin's sharp brown face. It was as if he thought his words were so obvious that they were hardly worth saying.

'But nobody can become a bird!' said June.

He looked at her very seriously. 'It happened to you. You decide if it was real or not.'

June looked at the beautiful blue statue — the talisman. Even the word was strange: talisman .... She stroked it. It was hard and cold to the touch. It seemed to possess mysterious power; touching it was frightening, like standing beside a bottomless well.

She realised that she had first noticed her ability to talk to birds some time after returning the talisman to Shahin. To return it, she had had to touch it. Could it be that its power had rubbed off on her? Was that why Shahin didn't like people touching it?

But Jennifer Adams had touched it too, and she couldn't understand the language of the birds. Something else had happened to her, though. Her whole personality had changed. Since that day, Jennifer had been no fun to be with. Could this carved piece of stone have so much power?

It glittered magically. It didn't seem to reflect light so much as to radiate its own light from within. Strange shapes appeared to move within it, playing upon June's imagination. It was like gazing into another world.

'Do you know anyone with spiky red hair?' Shahin's

voice intruded on her thoughts. He, too, was staring at the talisman.

'Yes. Nodser. The fella I was telling you about, who wants to take Longwing.'

Something gripped June's stomach tightly: fear. The strange shapes she had imagined she saw in the talisman — had that been Nodser stealing Longwing from her house?

Or did June just think that because Shahin had asked her about someone with spiky red hair? Why had he asked her that? And what was he doing? He had picked up the talisman and was holding it as if he was trying to sense something from it with his finger-tips. The shapes still glittered within it, but June couldn't read them any more.

There was a knocking sound at the window.

'Go away, stupid bird!' Shahin shouted. 'Look. Now a pigeon has decided to disturb me.'

June looked out the window. A pigeon was walking back and forth on the ledge, like an electronic toy. The green neck-feathers beneath its nodding head glittered like tinsel. It stopped and pecked urgently at the glass. It was Supersonic.

'Supersonic! It's Supersonic. What's he —'

She rushed to the window and opened it. Supersonic looked around the kitchen, turning his head as if it were on a swivel, but he didn't jump inside.

'Supersonic! What are you doing here?'

He stared at her. He seemed to be trying to remember something.

'What does he want?' Shahin was standing at June's side.

'Shhh. Listen,' she said.

'I can't — open — the ropes,' Supersonic was saying. 'Go — get June — go — Supersonic — fly — to the sea

— opposite a — round tower — the house — on the corner —'

'He is describing this address.'

'I left a note for Gerry saying I was coming here. It's a message from Gerry.'

'Tell her — comequickJune. ComequickJune. ComequickJune.'

Supersonic swivelled his head from side to side, and when he seemed satisfied that June understood, he spun into the air and burst past the cherry blossom. He was out of sight even before the sound of his wingbeats vanished, and only the sweet melody of the garden birds remained.

'That is a very fast pigeon,' said Shahin. 'Very fast.'

Shahin spoke perfect English, but he had a way of mirroring the meaning of his words with his way of saying them; and this, with his Indian accent, meant that 'very fast' was said very quickly and pronounced 'verrifast'. If he had said Supersonic was 'very funny', he would probably have laughed while saying 'verrifunny'.

They were running towards the door when Shahin stopped and began to tap the pockets of his trousers. He had a dismayed look on his face. 'I am always doing this. I am always doing this! Keys, keys, keys,' he began to whisper, as if he hoped his keys would answer. He began to search behind cushions on the chairs, and amongst the bowls of knick-knacks on the kitchen counter.

June was in an awful position. She had seen his keys in the cupboard, but she couldn't just say, 'Look in the cupboard,' because Shahin might guess she had been snooping. But if she didn't say something, they might be too late to help Longwing. Annoyingly, Shahin showed no signs of looking in the cupboard.

'Why don't you look in the talisman?' June said.

'The talisman ....' He shook his head sadly. 'It would show me the keys lying in some corner, but it would not show me which corner. The talisman does not believe in helping me if I mislay something through my own stupidity. It is most unfair.' And he began up-ending bowls and flinging cushions onto the floor.

'Well, look in the cupboard,' said June impatiently.

'The cupboard. Good idea. Good —' Shahin opened the cupboard. 'Hey presto! How did you get here?' He grabbed the keys. 'I think you are psychic, June. Let us go.'

And they ran outside to Shahin's car.

A Brave Deed

Shahin's car was painted blue with yellow sunflowers, and it was covered in a very fine dust. Shahin tut-tutted angrily at this, but when June told him the dust came from the Sahara Desert he seemed happy.

The car was a Citroen 2CV, a little car with a curved roof which Shahin drove as if it were a Ferrari. (It's a French car, and the French call it a 'deux chevaux', which means 'two horses', because it has a two-horsepower engine.) He kept up a steady conversation with June, and also with every other driver on the road. It didn't matter if they were driving articulated lorries or double-decker buses; Shahin would not give an inch. His transformation from the gentleman he had been in his own house was startling. Once, June had gone with Gerry to watch her father play football — it had been one of the most boring afternoons of her life — and as soon as he had pulled on a pair of football boots, Ben had instantly turned into something like a rabid dog. Shahin wasn't that bad. But it was close.

June was giving directions, and this allowed her to bring up a subject she was very nervous about. 'I live in Ratheane Road. Ours is the last house on the road. My friend Jennifer Adams lives next door.'

Eeeeezzzzchhh!

Shahin had put his foot hard on the brake. All over the road, people in cars and lorries honked and howled and rolled down their windows and roared abuse at Shahin's crazy driving. You can't roll down the windows of a 2CV, so Shahin contented himself with shouting back through the glass — at about ten times the volume he had used when he was shouting at the blackbirds.

'Jennifer Adams? Do you notice any change about her recently?' Shahin looked as if the answer was a life-or-death issue for him.

June thought hard — not easy to do, under Shahin's wild stare. 'She cut her fringe last week.'

'I don't mean her *hairstyle*! Has her *personality* changed?'

'Sorry, you didn't say —'

'*Has it*?'

'Yes!'

'How?'

'She — she used to be really wild, but then she — became so sensible all of a sudden. It was unbelievable.'

'Aaahhh!' Shahin contorted his face horribly and banged on the hooter again and again. Then he realised he was doing it, stopped and said 'Aaahhh!' again. 'I have done that girl a great injustice. Remember that day when both of you came to see me, and she grabbed my talisman and ran off with it when I was not look-ing? She was going to stuff it up the exhaust pipe of a bus. A *bus*! I *hate* buses! She offended the falcon — my talisman.'

He suddenly lowered his voice. 'I put a spell on her.'

'You what?'

'I put a spell on her. I cursed her with sensibleness. I took away the best part of her spirit — her sense of fun. To remove the spirit of a living thing is a terrible deed. It is one of the three most terrible curses. And she is so young!'

Shahin thought for a moment. 'It is different with the others — they were old enough to know better,' he said with venom. 'But to her I have done a great injustice.'

'Can you not take the spell off?'

'No, I cannot!' he cried, and banged on the hooter again. 'I can do nothing for her! She must remove the spell herself, by performing a brave deed in the service of another. That is the only way out. And without her spirit, performing a brave deed is like — is like —' Again his voice went very low. '— is like a photograph escaping from a jar of its own accord.' Tears glistened in his eyes. He seemed to be in physical pain. 'I have done Jennifer a *great* disservice.'

'She does seem to be getting her sense of fun back,' June said, remembering what Jennifer had said to Sian Whelan about needing to get her head examined. She was desperate to cheer Shahin up. He looked ready to die of grief.

'Is she? She's getting back her sense of fun? Ah, that is very good. Very good. Oh yes.' Shahin's sorrow vanished as quickly as it had appeared. He pulled the car out onto the road and drove off, whistling.

Shahin explained to June that people cursed with sensibleness never do brave deeds in the service of others, because they are too dull and cautious. This is what makes the curse so vicious. First the victim must get his sense of fun back, ever so slightly, and that will allow him to do the deed. But Shahin said that, if you lose your sense of fun after reaching a certain age (around seventeen, he thought), it tends to stay lost. Sometimes people get it back again in their seventies, because they've got a little bit of wisdom by then. With children, too, the chances are good.

June asked him about something he had said earlier — about 'the others' being old enough to know better. What others?

Shahin told her he had put the spell of sensibleness on two other people since he had come to Ireland, two years before. One was a newspaper journalist who had visited Shahin, then written an article ridiculing him and his method of telling the future. The journalist, in his opinion columns, tried to tell the future by using social studies and economics and politics; but he wasn't half as accurate as Shahin was using his talisman — so Shahin said. (June reckoned that was the photograph she hadn't recognised.)

The other person was a politician who, after going to see Shahin, had demanded that he come to work for his party as a 'research assistant'. The politician said that, if Shahin refused, he would introduce a law that every fortune-teller had to pay a licence fee of five thousand pounds. Shahin had done neither; instead, he had put a spell on the politician.

Shahin explained that it was the power of the talisman that allowed him to put such spells on people. Because it had such power, he could have made a huge amount of money charging rich people a fortune to tell their fortunes. But he believed that something of such power should be within the reach of everyone; that was why he had chosen to work in a little shopping arcade (until it was closed down), charging people very little money.

And that was why paying a five-thousand-pound licence fee was out of the question.

Shahin felt that the two men were surely cursed for life, because they would never perform brave deeds in the service of others. The newspaper columnist probably wouldn't mind, Shahin said; his career had gone from strength to strength since he had become dull and sensible. But the politician's career had been ruined. If there's one thing people hate, it's a sensible politician.

☆

It was ten in the morning when they pulled up outside June's house. The front door was open, and as June and Shahin approached they heard Supersonic inside.

'Good riddance. Better off without her, Gerry. Better off,' he was saying.

Then they heard a muffled voice — Gerry's: 'Ha wope! Hull ha wope!'

'I'm *pulling* it!' Supersonic said. 'I don't have a beak like a bullfinch's.'

They ran in. They found Gerry trussed up like a turkey on the kitchen floor. There were ropes tied around his ankles and wrists, and a cloth gag on his mouth. Supersonic was tugging half-heartedly at the rope on Gerry's wrists.

June rushed to Gerry and undid the gag from his mouth. There was an ugly red bruise on his jaw.

'June, you'll never *believe* what's happened.'

'What?' June asked. Shahin was untying the knots on Gerry's wrists and ankles.

'I can talk to Supersonic! You do it with your mind, don't you? You have to get on the same wavelength as him. I mean, I'm not as good as you are — I'm not a natural, it's really hard — but I did it! I sent Supersonic to get you! With a messa —'

'*Gerry*!'

'Yeah?'

'What happened?'

Gerry looked at Shahin untying the last knot from his ankles. 'Oh yeah. Nodser called round. I wouldn't let him in. So he went next door, took the ladder from Jennifer Adams, and climbed up to my window. He's *mad*, he is! Then he punched me and tied me up and let himself out the front door.'

June and Shahin looked at each other. 'It is as I saw,' Shahin said.

'He took Longwing,' Gerry continued.

'Good riddance,' said Supersonic. 'Better off without her. Falcons — who needs them?'

'We all need falcons,' said June. 'They saved the world once.'

'They might have saved it, but the pigeons own it.' Now that Longwing was gone, Supersonic's old cockiness had returned. He sang, 'Pigeons, pigeons everywhere.'

'Supersonic, shut up,' said June.

'Where is your room?' asked Shahin.

'Pigeons in the park and pigeons in the air!

Pigeons on street-corners,

Pigeons sitting on top of your car ....'

Supersonic sang to the now-empty kitchen. The humans had run upstairs to June's room.

☆

Nodser had climbed in through Gerry's window, which stood open for Supersonic, and then gone to June's room. There were signs of a struggle — or, rather, there were signs of a man chasing a falcon around the room. The quilt was on the floor, and the bedside lamp had been knocked to the ground. There was no sign of Longwing.

'I dunno where he took her,' Gerry said.

'Uncle Jack,' said June. 'He'd know. We'll ring Uncle Jack.'

They rushed down to the kitchen, where Supersonic was happily munching from a bowl of salted peanuts and taking the odd slurp from a saucer of Coke. June rang Uncle Jack on his mobile phone. He was making a delivery in his van, down the country. First he was raging that Nodser had stolen the falcon. Then he was disappointed that June wasn't going to sell the falcon, and a bit surprised at her surprise that he should even think of such a thing. (June could not imagine that she had ever wanted to sell a falcon.)

Uncle Jack had no idea where Nodser might have taken Longwing. But he warned June not to try anything. He would be around in two hours. Nodser was dangerous.

☆

Gerry made tea and scrambled eggs for everyone. In fact, he, not June, had been doing most of the cooking since their parents went away. This morning he melted cheddar cheese into the eggs and sprinkled them with black pepper and herbs. Neither June or Shahin said anything, or even seemed to notice what they were eating.

Nodser might have taken Longwing anywhere. He had put her in a cardboard box and disappeared. In their rush to leave Shahin's house, June and Shahin had left the talisman behind, so they couldn't use it to help them find her. By the time they drove all the way back to the house, it might be too late. But that was what they were going to have to do. And even then, Shahin said, it might just show them Longwing in a cardboard box, without showing where the box was.

June thought her heart would break. Not only did she think it was all her fault, but, since the night before, she could feel what Longwing felt. She could feel her captivity, and her loneliness at being separated from Bluebeak and her territory. June was desperate to find her. She couldn't keep still for two seconds.

They were finishing the scrambled eggs when they heard a deafening wolf-whistle from the front of the house. It sounded like a sailor at a Miss World contest. 'Oy!' shouted a voice. 'June!'

Someone ran in the front door and burst into the kitchen. It was Jennifer Adams.

'What's the story?' she shouted. 'Stuffing your faces when someone's stolen your falcon! Aren't you gonna go get the bird?'

Jennifer had an enormous violet bruise around her right eye, and her lilac-patterned dress was torn and covered in oil stains.

'Did you say "falcon"?' said Shahin.

'Hey, look,' said Jennifer, grinning, 'it's Mr Fortune-Teller. Looked into your crystal thingy lately?'

'All the time,' said Shahin.

'Jennifer, what happened?' asked June.

'I was in the garden next door, and in comes this weedy-looking bloke wanting to know if he could borrow my ladder.'

'Nodser,' said Gerry.

'Nodser is right. He had something tattooed on his forehead. I was trying to read what it said. It was tiny. Why get a tattoo if no one can read it? Anyway, it said, "What you looking at?" Then he bopped me in the eye with it. This is one serious black eye, am I right or am I wrong or am I right? Next thing I know, he's strolling out your front door with a box. So I ran at him.'

'Jennifer!' said June.

'I ran at him, but he shouted at me to keep away. He said there was a valuable bird in the box and if I didn't want to be responsible for its death I'd mind my own business.'

'And what did you do?' asked Shahin.

'As you well know, Mr Fortune-Teller,' said Jennifer casually, 'I was never any good at minding my own business.' June couldn't believe the way she was behaving. This was the old Jennifer come back. She continued, 'I jumped on his back fender and held on, that's what I did. He didn't see me. Anyone ever ride across the city holding on to the back of a van? I recommend it. Interesting, to say the least — especially the sharp corners, and the looks people give you when you're stopped at traffic lights.'

'Where did the van go?' June asked.

'To a warehouse down by the docks. It's locked, by the way. And we'd better get there quick. They're putting the falcon on a ship going to Arabia tonight. I heard Nodser telling another bloke as thick-looking as himself. I saw a toy car outside. I presume that's the fortune-teller's.'

'Shahin is my name,' said Shahin.

'Jennifer is mine,' said Jennifer. 'We've met before.'

'Indeed,' said Shahin.

'Well, let's get motoring. We can't sit around here all day making small talk. Let's hit the docks!'

☆

On the way to the car, June whispered to Shahin, 'The spell has lifted.'

'So it would appear,' murmured Shahin.

'She did a brave deed for me, and the spell has lifted.'

Shahin looked at June, and for the first time that day she sensed disapproval in his eyes. 'She did a brave

deed in the service of a falcon,' he said. 'It is wrong to think of ourselves all the time.'

They walked out to the car, and all of them — June, Shahin, Gerry and Jennifer — piled in. Shahin started the engine, and they were flung from side to side, as if on a roller-coaster, as the little car hurtled towards the docks.

☆

Two hours later, Uncle Jack pulled up to the house and found it empty of people. He looked in the kitchen window and saw Supersonic on top of the fridge — once again the top bird in the house. If Jack could have understood, he would have heard Supersonic singing:

'Pigeons, pigeons everywhere,
Wherever you go, there's a pigeon there.
How *do* they do it? The devil may care.
A thousand pigeons in Pigeon Square.
YO!
Hello there, Jack-beyond-the-window.'

Down by the Docks

~

At the port, a ship with Arabic lettering on the side was docked under a giant loading crane. A container the size of June's house was being hoisted onto it. Overhead, black-backed gulls wheeled and banked against the pale blue sky.

After they had travelled along the river for half a mile, Jennifer had Shahin drive through a maze of side-streets until they came to the run-down but very solid-looking warehouse where she said Nodser had taken Longwing. There was a yard behind the warehouse, full of rolls of black plastic piping which dwarfed the car.

They drove into the yard and up to the great doors. There were no people or cars around. Old warehouse areas down by the docks are among the few places in the city that can be totally empty of people during the day.

They got out of the car. As Jennifer had said, the doors of the warehouse were locked.

'She is inside,' said Shahin.

June was trying to find a crack in the doors. 'How do you know? I can't see anything.'

'I can smell her.'

'We all know you have a great big hooter, but it's hardly big enough to smell a falcon through a concrete wall,' said Jennifer.

'I can, and if you will please clear the snot from your nose sometime, perhaps you will smell her too,' Shahin replied.

Jennifer's hand shot up to her nostrils. There was no snot there, but her face reddened and she went quiet.

'What are we going to do?' asked Gerry.

'Smash the lock,' said June.

Shahin touched the padlock. 'This could serve as an anchor for a small ship. I'm afraid we are not going to be smashing this today.'

'Well — get the key,' June suggested desperately.

'Where?' Gerry asked.

June looked at Shahin, then at Gerry and Jennifer. When no one said anything she set off, half walking, half running, around the warehouse. The others followed at a slower pace. They found one other entrance, a smaller side door, also padlocked.

'We will wait for this Nodser person,' said Shahin, when they arrived back at the main doors.

'If he sees us, he might not come in,' said Gerry.

'Of course he'll come in. He has to get Longwing,' said June, standing solidly with her fists clenched. She was in the mood to fight someone.

'What we will do is drive in behind the rolls of piping and surprise him when he comes to collect Longwing,' Shahin said calmly. He turned to walk towards the car.

'I say we pick the lock with a hairpin. That's what they do in films. I've done it myself a few times,' Jennifer put in. She'd got over what Shahin had said about the snot.

Shahin stopped and looked around. 'Do you have a hairpin?'

Jennifer shook her head. Shahin said, 'Well then,' turned, and climbed into the car.

'Anyway, you'd need a crowbar to pick this lock,' said Gerry.

Shahin started the engine of the car. As there were no crowbars around, there was nothing to be done except get in, drive behind the rolls of piping, and wait.

The waiting was agony for June. She wasn't sure that Shahin's sense of smell was actually so strong that he could smell Longwing. She wouldn't have been surprised if he had animal-like powers, but she thought that maybe he had another sense in addition to sight, hearing, touch, taste and smell.

She thought so because she could sense Longwing close by. Feeling this and not being able to do anything about it was torture. June wanted to go out and kick down the doors of the warehouse, but she had to be patient. She wondered if Longwing could sense her presence and take comfort from it.

When June had been a falcon, in the night, she had given no thought to the future until she began to miss her own body. What if Longwing had no thought for the future? What if she thought the present — being locked in a box — was how it was always going to be? The idea drove June crazy. She couldn't sit still or join in the others' conversations. She began to get irritated that they could laugh and tell jokes at a time like this.

After two hours of waiting, Shahin suggested to June that she should go and get food. She said that she wasn't hungry, and that even if she was she wouldn't leave the warehouse. Jennifer, her eye now purple and swollen, wouldn't go either, in case anything happened while she was away.

Gerry went. His jaw was as purple and swollen as Jennifer's eye, but while she proudly examined her bruise in the car mirror, he hardly seemed to notice his. June's nervous fidgeting was beginning to get on his nerves; he was glad of a chance to get away.

Shahin gave him money to buy food for everyone. June wanted chips with garlic dip, chicken nuggets with salt, and a can of orange. Shahin wanted chips and fresh whiting, with vinegar but no salt (too much salt is very bad, he said), and a mineral water. Jennifer wanted curry chips with lots of salt and vinegar, a cheeseburger and a Coke. Then Shahin wondered if he wanted sauce, either garlic or curry, with his chips; he seemed a little disappointed, even angry, when no one in the car could tell him if he did or not. Jennifer, in light of what Shahin had said, decided she didn't want as much salt — just a little bit — and could she change that cheeseburger to a spiceburger? There was no pen or paper for Gerry to write the orders down. June wanted to know what whiting was like — was it more like fresh cod than fresh plaice? If it was, she wanted whiting, but if not she'd stick with the chicken nuggets — but could she change the orange to mineral water?

Gerry listened to all this without saying a word, got out of the car, and came back half an hour later with four portions of smoked cod and chips and four cans of Coke. The look on his face as he handed around the brown paper bags cut short any arguments, and the meal was eaten in stony silence.

Even though June had said she wasn't hungry, she ate all her fish and chips — partly because it gave her something to do. It was Gerry, the one who had gone to get the food, who ate least. This was normal for him; he had a poor appetite. Shahin, who had a very big appetite, finished Gerry's portion, and this brought Gerry back into the fold after the tension caused by his ignoring the others' orders.

☆

Sunny afternoon grew into shadowy evening. No one came to the warehouse. The car was parked in an avenue between the rolls of piping. At one end of the avenue they could see the warehouse door; at the other end, a wire mesh fence separated the yard from a patch of waste ground. Bushes and weeds grew there, and birds flew to and fro on urgent bird business. Was it possible to become a bird, June wondered? Had she become one last night? Could it be done at will?

What if Nodser used the side door?

The thought struck her tummy like a thunderbolt.

'What if he uses the side door? *He might have been here already!*'

Everyone froze.

'He'd still have to come into the yard by the main entrance,' Gerry said.

'Yes,' Shahin said, 'he would.' He sounded relieved.

A light flickered on the wall of the warehouse, and with a screech of brakes Nodser's blue van pulled into the yard and stopped outside the doors.

He was out of the van almost before it had stopped, striding calmly towards the doors. It was obvious he had no idea he was being watched. He stood in front of the padlock for a minute; it must have been stiff, because he stepped away from the doors and gave them three vicious kicks. They didn't budge.

He started on the locks again. Thirty long seconds passed; then he pushed the doors with both hands, and each one in turn opened inwards, as if they were reluctant horses that had to be shoved into their stable.

Nodser went back to the van. He was limping badly on the foot he had kicked the door with. In the dusk, the four people waiting in the car could barely make out his bristly red face, contorted with pain and fury. He climbed into the van. The lights came on and were swallowed up by the great black hole of the doorway. The van followed the lights into the warehouse.

Shahin turned the key in the ignition but didn't switch on the lights. He pulled on the gear stick, and they too were rolling into the vast warehouse.

Nodser, blinded in the beam of his own headlights, stood holding a cardboard box. He had been walking towards his van when Shahin drove in. Shahin stayed outside the full flood of the van's lights. The four of them got out of the car.

'Who's they *are*?' Nodser shouted.

'Hand over that falcon, sir!' Shahin ordered.

'Says *who*?'

'My name is Shahin.'

'Well, that's your prob*lem*, *pal*. My prob*lem* is, I have to put this *boird* on a *boat*. So, like, get *lost*, Shahin. Nice to meet*ya*.'

'What you are doing is against the law. Hand over the falcon, Mr Nodser, or I will be forced to take her from you.'

'You an' whose *army*, like?'

'*This* army!' Jennifer roared.

'This army!' Gerry shouted.

'Give me back Longwing!' said June.

Nodser's mouth twisted into a gummy grin. 'Is the *crèche* not open to*day*, or wha'? No *dolls* to play with?'

Shahin stepped into the beam of the van's headlights. 'Please hand over —'

'*Hey-look-out-he's-got-a-gun*!' yelled Gerry.

Instantly, almost as if he'd been expecting this, Shahin stepped back into the darkness. Nodser pointed a squat little pistol — so toylike it had to be real — in their general direction. Because of the glare of the headlights, he couldn't make them out clearly. Shahin drew June, Gerry and Jennifer further into the shadows.

Nodser edged towards the van. 'Appreciate your concern for the *boird*.' He opened the door and put the cardboard box in the passenger seat. 'Coming down here to wave her *off*, like. *Very*, very *thoughtful*, I must *say*.' Nodser's grin had become a mocking, twisting sneer. He turned to climb into the driver's seat.

'Look out, June! Come back!' shouted Gerry.

But June was gone. All the frustrations of the day had exploded. She was racing down a red tunnel of rage towards Nodser. Gerry and Jennifer started after her. June was on him, punching, kicking; but Nodser laughed, effortlessly avoided her with a boxer's side-step, locked one arm around her throat — and she was trapped, unable to speak, with Nodser's gun pointing at her head.

'Get back!' he snarled.

Gerry and Jennifer were rooted to where they stood, afraid to make the slightest movement in case it tipped Nodser over the edge.

'Don't hurt her, Nodser!' Gerry pleaded.

'That's *better*,' said Nodser, through clenched teeth.

Gerry and Jennifer disappeared. Silently, swiftly, like a ghost, Shahin had stepped forward and whisked them back into the darkness.

'Where did they *go*?' Nodser asked June, as if he wasn't holding a gun to her head. Where did they go? She didn't know. She couldn't say. She could hardly breathe.

The warehouse was deathly quiet. June couldn't believe someone was holding a gun to her head. It was too like a film to be real. She wanted to laugh.

A ridiculous thought struck her: had Gerry got garlic sauce with the chips? No. It was Nodser's breath that smelt of garlic. She could feel it hot on the tip of her left ear.

It didn't seem like a film any more. The slightest pressure of Nodser's finger on the trigger, and she would be dead.

Something flew upwards out of the shadows — June heard it more than saw it. There was a deafening crash by her right ear, and an orange flash streaked towards the warehouse roof. An electric buzzing sounded in June's head. Nodser had fired his gun at the thing that moved.

He was no longer holding her by the throat. He had taken a step away, but he was still pointing the gun at her face. He was very nervous. June could hear his heart pounding. Or was that her heart?

'I'm going to drive outa here with the *boird*. No one try to *stop* me. And no one gets *hurt*. All righ'?' Nodser waited for a reply, but all he got was his own echo, followed by the silence of a tomb. He began to edge slowly towards the van again.

The warehouse ceiling was as high as a church. Suddenly, from out of its darkness, a lump of metal fell on Nodser's wrist, and the gun went clattering across the concrete floor. Nodser screamed in pain and clutched his wrist. The lump of metal, instead of crashing to the floor with the gun, swooped upwards like a paper aeroplane, making an arc in the light, and came rushing back at Nodser's face. It was a peregrine falcon.

The bird's vicious talons drew red streaks on Nodser's face. A dark jet of blood sprayed the windscreen of the

van. Nodser screamed and bent double to protect his head.

The falcon swooped upwards and again stooped at him. The blow knocked him over. He got up on all fours and stumbled and ran and crawled, like a desperate, wounded animal, out through the warehouse doorway. For a few seconds, his screams echoed around the warehouse; then they too fled into the dusk. The falcon had flown after him.

With hands that wouldn't stop shaking, June reached into the van and grabbed the cardboard box. She was crying. She ripped off the tape and opened the box.

Longwing blinked in the sudden light and looked around with jerky motions of her head. 'I knew you would come, June,' she said.

'Longwing!' Longwing jumped out of the box and onto June's arm. 'Longwing.' June burst into tears. She couldn't stop herself. Sobs like hiccups wracked her body. She had been so frightened, and she was so happy to see ....

But — the other falcon? June looked around, and her sobs were replaced by snuffles.

Gerry and Jennifer raced to her.

'Wow!'

'Are you all right, June?'

'The gun!'

'Where'd that bird come from?'

'The shot!'

'Did you *see* that?'

'He had a gun on you! You'll be on television.'

Their voices trailed off. Longwing perched on June's arm, and with her other hand June stroked the falcon's head. Having just witnessed the stunning power of a peregrine, Gerry and Jennifer were awed at the tenderness between them. Longwing and June murmured to each other. Gerry felt a shiver go down his spine, so far away from the human world did his sister seem. He couldn't understand what they were saying, even though he had managed to get close to Supersonic's wavelength.

After a time June came out of the daze and looked around. 'Where's Shahin?' she asked.

'He pulled us back to the wall,' said Gerry.

'Told us to keep quiet,' said Jennifer.

'He just disappeared. He was really weird. Shahin!' Gerry shouted.

'Shahin ... shahin ... in ... in ....' shouted the echo.

'Where did the other bird come from?' Jennifer asked.

'It must have been Bluebeak, Longwing's mate,' said June.

'Bluebeak guards our territory,' Longwing said.

'What?' said June.

They heard footsteps in the doorway. Shahin walked in. His black eyes looked vacant, and this, with his hooked nose, made his face seem hard and cruel.

When he saw Longwing he stopped and slowly held out his arm. She flew to him. He stroked her head and she nibbled gently on his finger.

'Where did you disappear to?' asked Jennifer. 'The other bird — was that Longwing's mate?'

Shahin didn't reply.

June watched the way he spoke to Longwing. There was something very powerful about him.

Suddenly it struck her. He had turned himself into a falcon. He had attacked Nodser. He was able to do at will, or at times of great stress, what she had done in her sleep.

It was a crazy idea; but June was sure of it. Longwing had said Bluebeak was guarding their territory. Shahin had turned himself into a falcon.

Shahin smiled. 'I do not think the pigeon Supersonic would thank us for bringing this magnificent creature back to your house,' he said. 'You know, the night is so lovely, I suggest we take a drive down the coast — to Longwing's territory. Would you like to do that? We will bring that disgusting object with us.' He was looking angrily at the pistol on the floor.

The others were still shocked after seeing June held at gunpoint and Nodser knocked over by the peregrine. But all of them wanted to drive to Longwing's territory.

☆

On the drive, June, with Longwing on her lap, sat in the front. Gerry and Jennifer were in the back. June could feel Longwing's talons gripping sharply into her thighs every time there was a bump in the road, which was often. Once June had to prise the talons loose, so tightly did Longwing grip, and she felt blood on her fingertips.

When Gerry and Jennifer were talking to each other, June asked Shahin, very quietly, if he had become a falcon in the warehouse.

He shrugged his shoulders.

'Did you?' she whispered.

'According to you, that is not possible,' he whispered.

June smiled and whispered back, 'If you have the power of the talisman, anything is possible.'

She could see that Shahin, too, was smiling as he looked at the road. As he steered around a corner, he said, very quietly, 'Maybe the talisman turned itself into a live falcon. Maybe it was a living falcon once and can become one again when the need arises.' He was staring at the road ahead, grinning broadly.

June had never thought of this. Of course! That was

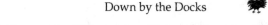

it! The talisman had become a living falcon and flown to the warehouse.

Shahin glanced at her. 'Then again,' he whispered, 'maybe not. Maybe it was me.'

Then the inevitable happened. Jennifer heard them.

'Oy! What's this? Whispering in the front? What's going on? Oy oy?'

Shahin laughed. He told them merrily of the second most terrible curse he knew — the ants-in-the-pants curse. (The worst one was too terrible to mention, he said.) To be cursed with not being able to sit still for two seconds at a time was even worse than being cursed with sensibleness.

'What's this curse of sensibleness?' asked Jennifer.

Shahin told her.

'Talk about a stupid curse,' she said.

'Take care it never happens to you,' he said.

'Some chance,' said Jennifer.

Shahin grinned and went on to tell them that, in their own self-satisfied way, people cursed with sensibleness are happy with it. But not being able to sit still for two seconds is unbearable. There is no relief, only exhausted sleep in the middle of the night when the body can take no more. And after an hour or two of nightmares, the sufferer is switched on like a radio alarm clock for another day of tormented motion. It sounded very like June's day had been since she had discovered that Nodser had snatched Longwing.

Shahin hinted strongly that this would be Nodser's fate for the rest of his days. Very seriously, he recited:

'Recognise the sunken eye,
The hollow cheek as they walk by.
By signals various we tell
The tortured soul in living hell,
For whom all-knowing fortune says,

"Wretched nights, tormented days."
Who steals the falcon from the sky,
Condemned to living, longs to die.'
When he finished there was silence, broken only by Jennifer saying, 'Boom-boom.'

June knew how close she had come to drawing this curse on herself. An idea struck her, one that she would write in her notebook: Shahin's curses involved changing the balance of people's own natures. A twist of the dial from wildness to sensibleness, and Jennifer had become almost a different person. Now the dial had gone back to wildness, and Jennifer had changed again. (June wondered if her photograph was now out of the jar in Shahin's cupboard.) A twist of the dial further along the ants-in-the-pants band, and Nodser would not be able to stay still for two seconds for the rest of his life. He would be in torment.

June wondered if she could use this knowledge to put curses on people she didn't like — Sian Whelan, for instance — but she immediately felt ashamed of having such an unworthy idea.

Another thought came to her. If she had gained her ability to talk to birds from touching the talisman, was the power permanent, or would she have to renew it through further contact with the talisman? She offered her finger to Longwing, who nibbled sleepily on it. At that moment, June could not imagine a time when she would be unable to understand birds. She would have to make sure the dial on her own nature stayed steady.

The car sped along the quiet coast road. June looked out at the ocean, swollen with the tide, and thought about the most incredible twenty-four hours of her life.

Dance of Love

~

Every living thing in the inlet was basking in Spring's victory. Flowers posted their scent on the night air; leaves bathed in the dew; and two peregrines flew across the face of the moon. The male falcon, the tiercel called Bluebeak, swooped down from their eyrie. The larger falcon, called Longwing, soared towards him. Bluebeak flipped upside down to grasp in his talons an object Longwing carried. It was a present from a girl called June, who lived — usually, but not always — in a world very different from his. She had bought it at a restaurant in a small town that was, unwittingly, part of the falcons' territory. It was a chicken nugget.

Four humans watched the aerial acrobatics from the coast road below. The air was so fresh and moist that, as they breathed it, they were reminded of drinking fresh water when they were parched with thirst. They were the she-humans June and Jennifer and the he-humans Shahin and Gerry. The he-human Shahin aimed, swung, and flung a metal object. It spun out into the swelling sea, which swallowed it up as easily as if it were a grain of sand. It was a gun.

Seven human eyes (one of Jennifer's was swollen shut) watched the sickle-shaped shadows twisting, turning, curving, looping, swooping in the night that was bright as day. And they knew that this was not a dance of death. This was a dance of love.

If you liked this book, you'll love

FOWL PLAY

the wild and wacky bestseller by
Jim Halligan and John Newman

The twins (super-messy Terry and her super-neat brother
Alex), and their eccentric friend Professor Miller, are on a
mission to save the world's rarest bird from extinction.

But unfortunately, Marcel La Bouche, the world's most
famous insane chef, and his sloppy sidekick Sam Biddle,
who kills chickens for fun, are on a mission too — and
they're bringing along their Plucking and Sucking Machine!

A fast, furious and funny adventure
for dodo-lovers everywhere!

ISBN 0-86327-639-3

New from Wolfhound Press!

millennium@drumshee

Drumshee Timeline Series Book 7

Cora Harrison

Emma doesn't care if Drumshee was once the family home;
she didn't want to move there anyway. She misses London,
her friends, her chess club .... The only good thing about
Drumshee is her German shepherd puppy, Heidi.

But then Emma starts playing chess on the Internet with
Bruce, an Australian boy in hospital after a surfing accident.
And when Bruce's father is accused of stealing a huge sum
of money, Emma will need all her chess skills
and her father's computer knowledge
to unravel the mystery and prove his innocence ....

A thrilling cyber-mystery
from the author of *Titanic — Voyage from Drumshee*!

Visit our website at

www.drumshee.com

ISBN 0-86327-715-2

Also Available from Wolfhound Press

Fionn the Cool

Aislinn O'Loughlin

When Cathy and Saoirse go to take a look at the statue
that has mysteriously appeared on O'Connell Street,
they don't expect to find themselves landed with two real
live Celtic teenagers who have been magically transported
from sometime BC to 1998!

And that's only the beginning. As well as helping the
obnoxious Prince Diarmuid and his sensible friend Fionn get
back home, the girls (with the help of weird Professor Keegan
and his solar-powered hologram camcorder)
have to find a way to get rid of the gorgeous but nasty
Cumac, who is plotting to kill the boys,
in this fast-paced and zany time-travel story.

The fifth book from teenage author Aislinn O'Loughlin,
whose off-beat alternative fairy tales have already won the
White Raven Award.

ISBN 0-86327-669-5

All books available from:
WOLFHOUND PRESS
68 Mountjoy Square
Dublin 1
Tel: (+353 1) 874-0354   Fax: (+353 1) 872-0207